PUFFIN BOOKS

M.I.HIGH

Secrets and Spies

D1322472

Books in the M.I. High series:

M.I. High: A New Generation
M.I. High: Secrets and Spies
The Official M.I. High Spy Survival Handbook

M.I.HIGH

Secrets and Spies

Adapted by Jonny Zucker

PUFFIN

PUFFIN BOOKS

Published by the Penguin Group
Penguin Books Ltd, 80 Strand, London WC2R 0RL, England
Penguin Group (USA) Inc., 375 Hudson Street, New York, New York 10014, USA
Penguin Group (Canada), 90 Eglinton Avenue East, Suite 700, Toronto, Ontario, Canada M4P 2Y3
(a division of Pearson Penguin Canada Inc.)
Penguin Ireland, 25 St Stephen's Green, Dublin 2, Ireland (a division of Penguin Books Ltd)
Penguin Group (Australia), 250 Camberwell Road, Camberwell, Victoria 3124, Australia
(a division of Pearson Australia Group Pty Ltd)
Penguin Books India Pvt Ltd, 11 Community Centre, Panchsheel Park, New Delhi – 110 017, India
Penguin Group (NZ), 67 Apollo Drive, Rosedale, North Shore 0632, New Zealand
(a division of Pearson New Zealand Ltd)
Penguin Books (South Africa) (Pty) Ltd, 24 Sturdee Avenue, Rosebank,
Johannesburg 2196, South Africa

Penguin Books Ltd, Registered Offices: 80 Strand, London WC2R 0RL, England

puffinbooks.com

First published in Puffin Books 2008
1

Text copyright © Keith Brumpton and Kudos Film & Television Limited, 2008
Photographs copyright © Kudos Film & Television Limited, 2008
BBC and the BBC logo are the trademarks of the British Broadcasting Corporation
and are used under licence. BBC logo © BBC 1996
Text adapted by Jonny Zucker
All rights reserved

Set in Helvetica Neue
Typeset by Palimpsest Book Production Limited,
Grangemouth, Stirlingshire

Made and printed in England by Clays Ltd, St Ives plc

British Library Cataloguing in Publication Data
A CIP catalogue record for this book is available from the British Library

ISBN: 978-0-141-32362-6

Contents

Nerd Alert

Chapter 1

A scrawny male figure with beady little eyes was hunched over a computer, smirking. Clicking a button on the mouse, he couldn't resist letting out a high-pitched snigger as an image of the British National Space Centre filled the screen. *Losers!* If only they knew the chaos that was about to start raining down on them any minute!

The shadowy figure sat back in his seat, rubbing his hands and waiting for the fun to begin. He was really going to enjoy this.

The National Controller of the Space Centre watched nervously as rows of white-coated technicians furiously inputted data into their machines. Satisfied that all was well, he shifted his gaze to the giant screen at the front of the Control Room. A picture of a huge upright rocket with flames burning from its engines greeted him.

The Controller adjusted his glasses anxiously and

3

dabbed his sweaty forehead with a handkerchief. Taking a deep breath, he allowed himself a smile. *So this was it!* Lift-off time for the brand-new, unmanned European TV satellite was just seconds away.

'Remote satellite launch,' he ordered, pacing across the floor. 'Commence final countdown!'

A robotic voice began the countdown.

'Ten . . . nine . . . eight . . .'

Numbers began appearing on dozens of screens around the Space Centre.

'Seven . . . six . . . fi– . . . *BEEEP!*'

The Controller felt his heart thump against his ribcage as the sudden beeping sound screeched through the Centre. Something was horribly wrong. Every one of the screens in the building had stopped, frozen on the number five.

'What's happening?' he shouted desperately, as technicians punched madly on their keyboards. The Controller felt a rise of panic. It looked like no one knew what was happening.

He watched as the screens started flashing red. A single word appeared:

HAZARD

The Controller frantically lunged towards a computer, pushing his senior technician out of the way. But nothing he saw there made any sense.

As a deafening alarm ricocheted around the room, the Controller desperately pounded at the keys, trying everything he knew to get the launch back on track.

But it was too late.

A second later, a giant explosion filled the screens around the Centre. The Controller and his technicians could only stare in horror as the rocket was engulfed in a huge fireball.

'Someone's hacked into the system!' the Controller yelled hysterically.

Without warning, the Control Room was plunged into darkness as the screens went blank.

And then an almost childish cartoon icon of a pink worm appeared, beaming down into the room. A sinister message curved around it:

MORE KAOS TO COME

The Controller held his hands up to his face, his breath quickening. This was too much. Who would want to destroy the satellite?

Back in his darkened den, the skinny male watched in delight as the Controller slumped, exhausted, into a chair at the Space Centre. He couldn't believe how the Centre's well-planned launch had been so easily terminated.

'Game over, suckers!' the figure cried victoriously, cheering at the computer screen. 'The Worm can never be defeated!'

The Worm attempted a cackle, but all that he could muster was a squeaky giggle. Oh well, there was time to perfect his evil laugh later – once he'd had more fun with the country's space programme!

M.I.HIGH

Chapter 2

Outside the gates of St Hope's School, Blane Whittaker and his best mate, Stewart Critchley, were busy discussing one of the main obsessions of Stewart's life – computer games.

The two friends couldn't be more different. With scruffy dark hair falling over his face, Blane looked like a bit of a rebel. His tie was at half-mast and he wore a T-shirt covered in badges over his regulation school shirt. As the owner of a black belt in martial arts, Blane was lean and muscled – in direct contrast to Stewart, who had yet to grow into his lanky frame. Stewart's blond hair had been cut by his mum and made him look like a total geek.

'*Queen Valhalla!*' Stewart was gargling, waving a CD in the air. 'Best action game ever . . .'

Blane tried to feign interest, but his mind was elsewhere. He watched as the students filed into the school, on their way to morning classes.

'But it's got loads of strategy in it as well . . .'

Stewart continued happily. 'It is *awesome*.'

Finally realizing his friend wasn't listening to a word he was saying, Stewart suddenly remembered something Blane had mentioned the day before.

'Still thinking about your brother?' he asked.

Blane nodded glumly. His older brother, Kyle, was in the British Army's Fifth Commando Regiment and Blane didn't see him for weeks, sometimes months, on end. He couldn't believe Kyle had to go back so soon.

'I'm going to the station at four o'clock to see him off,' he said absently.

'So he's definitely going back overseas?' Stewart asked, trying to be understanding. 'It's all part of being an army commando, I suppose.'

'It's no big deal.' Blane shrugged a little too casually. Even though Stewart was his best mate, he didn't want to admit to him how much he actually cared that Kyle was leaving today. 'He's always being sent off somewhere or other.'

Stewart looked thoughtful for a moment, but he was anxious to get back to his current favourite topic. 'So, Queen Valhalla,' Stewart was drooling, 'is, like, this total babe and she has a tribe of trolls who worship her.'

He stopped for a minute to gaze down at the image of Queen Valhalla on the front of the game.

With her horned Viking helmet and tiny outfit, she really was the ultimate honey of virtual warriors. Stewart smiled and looked up . . . just in time to spot St Hope's resident hottie, Daisy Millar, and her best friends, Kaleigh and Zara, walking by.

Stewart sighed deeply. In his vivid imagination, Daisy and Queen Valhalla had morphed into the same person. Stewart would have loved to talk to Daisy, but she was the kind of girl who'd never give him a second glance. He shook his head. He'd just have to stick with Queen Valhalla.

By late morning, it was time for their computer lesson and Stewart was positively itching to play *Queen Valhalla*.

Their teacher, Helen Templeman, was already sitting at her desk at the front of the room, working her way through her regular Mount Everest of papers.

The boys immediately plonked themselves down in front of the only working computer in the room and Stewart slipped *Queen Valhalla* into the CD drive. *Now for some action!*

Ms Templeman looked up from her books, just as a troll came crashing down on the head of an enemy trying to attack the rather skimpily-dressed female Viking warrior. A group of boys who had gathered round the computer whooped loudly. Ms

Templeman could feel the niggling symptoms of a migraine creeping up.

'All right, boys,' she said, trying to remain calm despite feeling anything but. 'Give someone else a chance.'

But the boys did what most of Ms Templeman's students normally did when she tried to assert her authority – they totally ignored her.

Ms Templeman sighed. She really needed the computer to be able to start the lesson. In typical St Hope's fashion, there was only one machine in the whole computer room that actually worked.

On the other side of the room, Daisy and Kaleigh watched the boys with disdain, while Zara got busy painting her fingernails. Who really cared about Queen Valhalla anyway? With her stupid sword and tiny little costume, she was hardly a fashion icon. Daisy scoffed – at least she knew how to put together an outfit properly.

Today was no exception. To Daisy, appearances were vital and she always added a touch of panache to her school uniform. Right now, she was wearing her favourite yellow waistcoat over her school shirt.

Crossing her arms, Daisy stared with incomprehension at the boys glued to the computer screen.

'What is it with boys and those dumb computer

games?' she groaned, turning back to Kaleigh with a scowl on her face. The two girls rolled their eyes. Boys just weren't interested in important things, like shopping or make-up application.

'Dorks versus Orcs,' Kaleigh added scornfully. 'So dull.'

At the mention of the word 'dull' Zara immediately looked up from her nails.

'Oh, d'you think so?' she asked, looking concerned. 'It says "Glitter Finish" on the bottle!'

Ms Templeman's increasingly urgent pleading interrupted the girls' conversation.

'Please, boys,' she begged, her voice rising several decibels in volume. 'The science group has some very important work to do!'

Ms Templeman was at her wits' end. Really, this computer room situation couldn't go on any longer. She would have to speak with the Headmaster about it.

The boys reluctantly moved away from the computer, muttering and groaning as Rose Gupta slipped into the vacant chair in front of the screen.

Unlike nearly all of her classmates, Rose stuck to the St Hope's dress code. It was partly because her father insisted, but mostly Rose just didn't see the point of the whole fashion thing. And so today she looked much the same as she did every day, with

11

her pristine school uniform neatly pressed. Rose also wore studious-looking glasses and had very shiny shoes.

She looked up as Stewart stuffed his copy of *Queen Valhalla* into his bag and sat down beside her. Rose might have spent a lot of time studying, but lately she'd started seeing Blane's geeky best friend in a different light. She could feel her cheeks burn. Stewart didn't seem to notice and just pulled out his notebook.

'How am I going to get to university using this pile of junk?' Rose muttered angrily, trying hard to hide her embarrassment. 'It's not as if it's any good, even when it is working. Only 32 meg. of RAM. What a joke!'

Stewart's ears pricked up. Rose definitely had a point – he couldn't even play *Queen Valhalla* properly on this machine.

'Don't even mention processor speed,' he grumbled.

'Power PC 603?' groaned Rose.

'ARM 32!' tutted Stewart in reply.

Across the room, Daisy was watching the exchange with interest.

'Nice flirty chat?' she called loudly, teasing Rose so all the class could hear.

'We were *just* talking about memory chips!' Rose

yelled back defensively. What was Daisy's problem? She could be so mean sometimes!

But Daisy wasn't about to let the class nerd off so easily.

'Right! So you might be joining his gaming club then?' she laughed.

Rose shook her head emphatically. She liked Stewart, but definitely not like that. Not that she'd ever admit to Daisy anyway. Besides, he didn't view computers in the same way as she did.

'Computers are for *scientific research*,' Rose called over to Daisy, ignoring Stewart's look of surprise. 'Not silly little computer games!'

Anyone watching the two girls throw comments back and forth across the classroom at each other would have been forgiven for thinking they were mortal enemies. But just outside, busy replacing the screws on a door hinge, was someone who knew very differently.

With his dirty overalls and worn brown jacket, Lenny Bicknall looked like any other school care-taker diligently going about his daily business. But right now Lenny had other business to take care of.

Looking around to make sure the coast was clear, Lenny flipped open the top of his screwdriver. Beneath it sat a small red button.

As Lenny pressed the button and hurried off down

the corridor towards his storeroom, something very strange was happening back inside the computer room of St Hope's.

Just as Ms Templeman clapped her hands together to indicate the start of class, Blane, Rose and Daisy saw the red eraser tips of their pencils starting to flash. Immediately hiding the red lights with their hands, the three excitedly caught each other's eyes.

It looked as though computer class would have to wait – they had far more important things to do.

M.I.HIGH

Chapter 3

Momentarily forgetting his melancholy, Blane's hand shot up. He had to get out of class right away.

'Yes, Blane?' sighed Ms Templeman. She was having a tough day. Judging from the science papers she'd been marking, she was beginning to wonder if any of her students listened in class at all.

'I need to go and feed Mr Flatley's tropical fish,' Blane said, smiling earnestly. 'He said he had a word with you?'

'He did, did he?' replied Ms Templeman uncertainly. She couldn't remember the conversation. But Blane was such a nice honest boy. 'OK . . . off you go then . . . but, do you know, I never even noticed he had an aquarium.'

Blane wasn't going to hang around to answer that one. He grabbed his things and made for the door.

Rose watched Blane go and instantly raised her hand too. She wanted to use a decent get-out line this time. Blane and Daisy were always getting in first, leaving her with the totally rubbish excuses. She was determined to impress Lenny today.

But, to Rose's despair, Ms Templeman had already spotted Daisy waving her arms around on the other side of the room.

'Daisy, are you helping with the fish too?' Ms Templeman said, looking weary.

Daisy pulled her best I'm-feeling-sorry-for-an-aged-relative expression.

'No, Miss,' she replied, her voice faltering with emotion. 'I have to ring Granny Millar; you know – the one in Australia. She's had a stroke and she can't talk right now. But Mummy says it would give her a big lift just to hear my voice.'

Daisy could see Ms Templeman's heart soften right in front of her. Secretly, she was proud of herself. Acting was Daisy's forte and she could turn on the sob story without even batting one of her long mascara-coated lashes.

'Off you go then,' nodded Ms Templeman sympathetically. 'And you give her my love.'

Daisy scooted out of the class. Of course there was no aged relative. The nearest she had been to Australia was seeing Rolf Harris at a book signing.

Rose could already feel herself blushing. How unfair was that? She'd been landed with the lamest excuse, *again*!

'Miss?' she said hesitantly. 'I need the toilet.'

The rest of the class sniggered as Ms Templeman gave her a worried look. Rose often had to leave class to use the toilet. Maybe something was really wrong with her. As Rose hurried out of the door, Ms Templeman wondered if she should talk to Mrs Gupta about it.

At the other end of the school, Rose found Daisy and Blane waiting for her outside a peeling blue door labelled 'Caretaker's Storeroom'. They nodded at her, tingling with anticipation.

Daisy reached out to the light switch and slid aside a panel, pressing the button underneath. A green light appeared, followed by a beeping sound. Checking the corridor to make sure no one was looking, Daisy turned the handle. The three teenagers filed quickly into the room and closed the door, trying not to knock over the paint tins, brooms and odd tools that were scattered around them.

Rose rushed straight over to a mop-head and pulled it towards her. A flashing green arrow lit up in front of an old paint tin on the floor. Daisy, Blane and Rose held their breaths.

A noise like a racing car accelerating in a Grand Prix tore through the room, as the floor seemed to give way beneath them. Hurtling downwards, the three teenagers could feel a massive rush of wind as their hair blew around wildly.

By now it's hopefully pretty clear that the St Hope's caretaker's storeroom wasn't just an ordinary broom cupboard. It was, in fact, a lift that – if you knew exactly which mop doubled as a lever to take you there – led to the top-secret headquarters of M.I. High, deep beneath St Hope's School.

And Daisy, Rose and Blane weren't just three typical teenagers. By the time they reached the bottom of the lift shaft, they'd been transformed into exactly what they'd been trained to be – M.I.9 secret agents, with stylish black trousers, tops and jackets to replace their uniforms.

Arriving at their destination, the three teen spies ran out of the parting doors as Lenny waited for them in the middle of the room. He was the one who had summoned them on their Pencil Communicators. He no longer looked like an anonymous school caretaker. His brown jacket and overalls had been replaced by a smooth purple suit, perfectly ironed shirt and his trademark polka-dot tie.

Pale yellow lights lit up the headquarters, and Lenny was standing in front of a curved workstation that housed technical equipment and three large plasma screens. Blane smiled – Ms Templeman would flip if she could see the number of computers here.

Without saying a word, Lenny indicated the middle screen to his agents. On it was an image of a satellite orbiting Earth.

'This is SPARTA, Britain's star wars defence satellite,' Lenny said. 'She orbits at a height of 39,000 kilometres, protecting the country from missile attacks.'

To demonstrate this, footage of an incoming missile appeared on the screen and it was arcing towards the Earth. But before it could make contact, shots fired out from SPARTA and the missile was blown into thousands of pieces.

'*Wicked!*' marvelled Blane, agog.

'Indeed,' Lenny agreed with a wry smile. Blane thought lots of things were 'wicked'. 'But SPARTA is old and needs to be replaced. In four hours her defence functions will cease. That's when the British National Space Centre will launch a rocket carrying her replacement. However . . .'

Lenny paused for dramatic effect. Daisy, Rose and Blane held their breath. They knew they had better listen up – this was going to be interesting.

'We seem . . .' Lenny continued, eyeing them gravely, 'to have a hacker.'

The four occupants of M.I. High HQ looked up at the screen as a worm icon suddenly appeared, along with the words 'MORE KAOS TO COME'.

'He calls himself "The Worm" and he's been infiltrating the Space Centre's computers. Our firewall experts have been unable to stop him.'

The three teen spies were deep in thought. Who did The Worm think he was?

Lenny reached for the remote. 'This was the launch of the European TV satellite. We lost our Uranus probe in the same way.'

The three agents jolted back in horror at the sight of the rocket erupting into a massive fireball.

Lenny guessed what they might be thinking. 'Luckily, both were unmanned,' he reassured them.

'But now you're worried The Worm will do the same to the SPARTA launch?' asked Rose, switching to mission mode. She still couldn't believe what she'd just seen.

Lenny nodded.

'That can't be allowed to happen,' he said, lowering his voice. 'M.I.9 believe a certain rogue state will attack Britain if they know SPARTA isn't in place to protect us. If the launch fails, then we may face an enemy attack within hours.'

The spies exchanged worried glances. This was going to be a deadly serious operation.

'Your mission is to find The Worm and stop him,' Lenny announced, finally revealing their assignment. 'The launch has to take place at four o'clock. You have four hours. Synchronize your watches.'

Three beeps sounded. As Daisy and Rose made their way over to the workstation, Blane approached Lenny carefully.

'Er . . . Lenny,' Blane began, nervously stepping forward. 'Four o'clock's a bit of a problem.'

Lenny locked eyes with Blane. It wasn't like him to try to get out of a mission. 'You've got something more important to do?' he asked sharply.

'Yeah . . . as a matter of fact,' replied Blane, frustrated that Lenny hadn't even waited for an explanation.

'More important than preventing a war?' Lenny asked him.

Blane was getting annoyed. Was this some kind of warped test? 'You've got Daisy and Rose to help you,' he pointed out, motioning to the girls.

'Listen, Blane,' said Lenny quietly, leaning forward until their faces were almost touching. 'You've got a key role to play.'

Lenny reached into his pocket and pulled out a small metallic blue device in the shape of a key-fob. It had a black-and-white football embedded in its centre.

'It's a computer tracking device to help locate The Worm,' he explained, passing the gadget to Blane.

The male agent turned the key-fob over in his hands. A series of triangles flashed around the perimeter.

'I had it specially done in the colours of your favourite team,' beamed Lenny, hoping they were about to come to an understanding. 'Leyton Orient, isn't it?'

Blane's eyes narrowed. How did Lenny know that? Even Blane's mum wasn't aware he still followed that hapless football team – his dad's treasured Leyton Orient. *Couldn't Lenny butt out just for once?*

'You really don't know anything about me!' Blane shouted angrily, storming off towards the lift. If he missed out on seeing Kyle, a stupid football key-fob was never going to make up for it. And besides, Lenny wouldn't know his Carl Griffiths from his David Beckham!

Within seconds the doors had closed and Blane was on his way back up to St Hope's.

Rose and Daisy were watching the commotion unfold, shocked. It wasn't like Blane to fly off the handle like that. Not at Lenny.

'He'll be all right,' said Rose, trying to convince herself as much as Daisy.

'He'd better be,' said Lenny darkly, walking over to them. They needed Blane to help them crack this mission. Otherwise, the whole of Britain could be in danger.

Upstairs, back in his school uniform, Blane saw he had a text message from Kyle.

'HEY BRO, GUESS YOU'RE IN CLASS RIGHT NOW,' he read. 'LOOKIN' FORWARD TO SEEING YOU LATER. MEANS A LOT TO ME – SEE YOU AT FOUR.'

Blane squared his shoulders defiantly. No matter what Lenny said, he was now more determined than ever to see Kyle. Worm or no Worm!

Chapter 4

Ms Templeman strode into the drab surrounds of the St Hope's staffroom and headed straight for Mr Flatley, who was in a corner delicately nibbling on his carefully quartered sandwiches.

'The kids are so desperate for some new computers,' she demanded, as the Headmaster looked at her sheepishly. 'I know we're strapped for cash, but what about the parents' fund?'

Mr Flatley continued chewing, moving his mouth from side to side like a particularly stunned cow. *Oh dear.* He should have been more prepared for this.

'Sadly, due to the activities of a corrupt few . . .' Mr Flatley swallowed nervously, putting down his sandwich and reaching for a brown envelope in the cupboard beside him. 'The parents' committee fund is actually *in the red* – at the moment.'

Ms Templeman looked suspiciously at the envelope as her boss handed it over. On the front were scribbled the letters 'IOU'. The teacher fished out the solitary piece of paper that was tucked inside: 'IOU £2,000'.

'We *owe* them two thousand quid?' she exclaimed.

'Yes.' The Headmaster forced a smile. 'But worry not! Mr Flatley has a plan.'

He picked up a packet of Rice Flakes breakfast cereal and passed it to the teacher. Ms Templeman took the box, slightly confused. She hadn't eaten yet, but this really wasn't her idea of a healthy lunch.

When she turned the cereal packet over, however, a smile of understanding crossed her face.

'"A set of brand-new computers to any school who can solve a simple maths problem and create a winning slogan",' she read out, breaking into a delighted squeal. 'That's great! But how simple is the simple problem?'

Mr Flatley pointed a thumb over his shoulder. 'The maths department is working on it now,' he smiled.

Behind him, an increasingly agitated teacher was trying to crack the problem on the staffroom whiteboard, but his efforts were clearly not bearing fruit. He threw the pen down and stomped off out of the door.

Ms Templeman frowned. The students badly

needed new computers. But if the maths department couldn't solve the problem, who could? Then a brainwave suddenly hit her.

She might not have returned from her toilet break this morning, but Ms Templeman knew she could always rely on Rose Gupta to rise to a mathematical challenge!

Rose and Daisy sat alone in M.I. High HQ, each taking their first steps towards solving the mission. Rose in particular was suffering from information overload. Thousands of complex letters and digits were scrolling furiously down her screen.

'Checking this data from the hacking attack is going to take hours!' she complained, leaning over to Daisy's screen. 'How's the profile going?'

'I reckon The Worm's a male,' Daisy mused. Her exceptional people skills made her something of an expert when it came to psychological profiles. 'I mean, check out the avatar,' she added, pointing at the worm icon.

'No girl would represent herself with a cartoon worm,' Daisy continued, scowling. 'I think we're looking at a real geek. The Stewart Critchley type. Hey! Maybe *you'd* fancy him!'

Rose closed her eyes and counted to three. She tried to ignore Daisy's catty remark.

'Where's Blane?' enquired Lenny, appearing from nowhere.

The girls looked away nervously. Blane's departure had put Lenny in a really foul mood.

'May I suggest one of you find him immediately and remind him of his duties?' Lenny commanded, turning on his heel.

The girls groaned. As if saving the world hadn't given them enough to do today!

At a wooden picnic table in the school quadrangle, Blane and Stewart had just finished their packed lunches.

'I'm skipping last period this afternoon to meet Kyle,' Blane was explaining.

'Oh yeah. I forgot about that,' Stewart said, looking like a neglected puppy. 'So, who am I going to play *Queen Valhalla* against?'

Blane shrugged his shoulders. 'I dunno. You'll have to find someone else.'

Stewart frowned. No one could match either him or Blane as champions of *Queen Valhalla*. And it would be too boring playing with anyone else – he'd just keep beating them all the time. Stewart packed his bag and trudged off glumly. There wouldn't be any more gaming today.

Blane was getting up just as Daisy sidled over.

Inside, Daisy's stomach was turning somersaults. She had to get Blane back on track as quickly as possible or Lenny would be causing humungous headaches for all of them. Not to mention The Worm totally jeopardizing the safety of the country.

'Hey!' she smiled. 'You lost your cool in there today. It must have been something pretty important.'

Blane looked at her like she was an idiot. He wasn't going to blab about his brother to Daisy, of all people.

'I thought this would be, like, your dream job?' Daisy went on softly, realizing something must be seriously up. 'Rockets, computer hackers, cartoon worms. How come you're trying to get out of it?'

Blane shook his head. 'You wouldn't understand. It's not kids' stuff.'

'Neither is this!' Daisy replied, suddenly frustrated. 'We have to make sure SPARTA gets launched or the country could be at *war*.'

Blane shot her a sullen look, so Daisy decided to change tack. She hated begging, especially to Mr Muscle. But there didn't seem to be any other option. She had to get Blane back on board, or there'd be trouble for all of them.

'Um . . .' she said quietly, swallowing her pride. Or at least pretending to. 'I don't think we can do it without you.'

28

There – she'd said it. He'd better go for it!

Daisy nervously kicked at the dirt. She was really playing the damsel-in-distress card and Blane looked close to relenting. Daisy took a breath and added the killer promise she knew he wouldn't be able to resist.

'You can have the special chair with the MP3 player and the drinks machine in the arm,' she offered, knowing Blane had been hankering after her M.I. High workstation chair for*ever*.

Blane's face slowly cracked into a hesitant smile as Daisy sighed with relief. How come the way to a boy's heart was nearly always through dumb gadgets!

'OK,' Blane agreed. 'But I definitely have to leave by three.'

On the other side of the school, Rose was also above ground and hurrying along the corridor. If Britain really was under threat, then she had to get back to M.I High HQ as soon as possible.

But Ms Templeman had other ideas. Spying her star pupil, she made a beeline for Rose.

'Ah, Rose, just the person!' Ms Templeman stopped Rose in her tracks.

Rose grimaced. As much as she liked her teacher, she didn't have time to chat right now. Not with The Worm on the loose.

'This is a competition to help the school win a fab set of computers – which we desperately need,' Ms Templeman was already gushing, rifling around on the top of her book mountain for something. 'All you have to do is complete the maths puzzle and then write a clever slogan. Aha, here it is!'

'I'm really busy today, Miss,' Rose replied frantically, crinkling up her nose.

Seeing Rose's expression, Ms Templeman silently wondered if Rose needed the toilet again.

'We're relying on you, Rose,' she smiled, not waiting for an answer as she pressed the form into her hands. 'And, er . . . the answer has to be in the post by tonight.'

Rose's heart sank. Where on earth was she going to find time to enter some dumb competition at a time like this?

Chapter 5

'That's The Worm?' asked Blane, slightly sceptical. 'He looks like Frankenstein's monster.'

Daisy, Rose and Blane were staring at the plasma screens in M.I. High HQ as a black-and-white composite image of several photos appeared.

'Look, even *I* wouldn't look good in a photofit,' Daisy retorted. 'But it's a start. I reckon we're looking at a young guy: brilliant, but with a big, big ego. The way he spells "KAOS" with a "k" tells me he's pretty immature, but dangerous, edgy and alternative. He probably doesn't just like hacking,' she added, staring at the picture thoughtfully. 'He probably likes blogs and gaming too.'

Blane had an idea. What was that new blogging site that Stewart had told him about? It sounded as though it was the type of place The Worm would hang out!

Blane tapped some keys and almost immediately the worm icon appeared. Too easy! If things kept going like this, they'd definitely finish the mission by four o'clock.

'Ha!' he shouted. 'There he is!'

'Once we get The Worm online, you need to keep him talking while I get a trace,' Rose instructed.

Blane began typing straight away, entering the chatroom under the name of Haxman. Trying not to be too obvious, he quickly zeroed in on the cyber-villain.

Hey, this is the Haxman, Blane keyed in, trying to sound casual.

Good to speak, Haxman, came the reply.

Wicked blog, mate, it's the best here by a mile.

The Worm thanks you.

'Keep him talking,' ordered Rose, frantically seeking a trace. She needed The Worm to stay online.

You and me we're into the same stuff, Blane continued, trying to remember some of the games Stewart was always going on about.

I don't think so. The Worm isn't playing games.

No, I know. I'd like to hack into all these amazing sites like you do.

The Worm doesn't call it hacking. He prefers the term 'Free Access'.

Rose madly scrawled through the hundreds of computer IDs coming up on her screen. She desperately needed more time!

The Worm needs to end this call. He has stuff to deal with.

Blane twitched nervously. If they couldn't get the trace, he could be stuck here all afternoon. Then he would have no one to blame for missing his brother except himself. He decided to make a drastic plug.

Maybe we could meet up sometime?
You ask The Worm too many questions. Ciao.

And with that The Worm was gone, just as suddenly as he'd appeared.

'Did you get a trace?' asked Daisy hopefully.

Rose shook her head despondently. They'd blown their only lead.

The Worm's spirits, however, were rising by the second. His fame was already spreading – even a newbie like Haxman knew who he was! Sitting in his lair, the master hacker took an enormous gulp of his drink through a straw and burped with satisfaction. Coupled with his green jumper and studious specs,

The Worm's bad table manners gave him the air of a precocious schoolkid.

'Excuse me! I heard that!' called a scolding voice from downstairs.

The Worm groaned inwardly. 'Excuse me, Mummy!' he called back meekly.

Turning back to his computer, The Worm grinned.

'Novices! Fools!' he cried, switching the display on his screen and smiling as a familiar Control Room came into view. 'Now to worm my way into the Space Centre!'

The Worm watched with amusement as an extremely jittery Controller appeared, looking exceedingly uncomfortable.

The truth was the Controller was on the verge of a nervous breakdown. The security of the country depended on the upcoming launch; he was beginning to feel terrified. He couldn't allow the new defence system to suffer the same fate as the TV satellite. It would completely ruin him – and possibly the entire country!

The Controller took a deep breath.

'Commence initial checks,' he commanded, watching the screen anxiously.

Little did he know The Worm was watching too.

Chapter 6

'Ah, Blane,' nodded Lenny, striding back to the workstation and noticing the male agent. 'Glad you decided to put the mission before your family matters.'

Still reeling from his encounter with The Worm, Blane spun round with shock on his face.

'You knew about me wanting to meet my brother?' he said incredulously.

'It's my job to know everything,' Lenny reminded him. 'Oh, and the Prime Minister wants an update. How's the mission going?'

The three teen agents avoided Lenny's gaze. They didn't have to tell him they were back at square one.

'That good, eh?' asked Lenny sarcastically. 'Right, you better keep at it then.'

'What was all that about?' Daisy whispered as soon as Lenny was out of earshot.

'Nothing,' shrugged Blane, unwilling to betray his hurt. 'It's too late now.'

'Too late for what?' asked Daisy, pressing the point. 'I didn't know you had a brother.'

Great! Thanks for nothing, Lenny, Blane thought. It didn't matter. Daisy wasn't going to let up anyway.

'He's in the Fifth Commando Regiment,' Blane replied, letting out a deep sigh. 'I don't get to see him much, but I was supposed to be seeing him off from the station at four. He's going away on military manoeuvres.'

So this was what all the fuss was about. Daisy could totally get why Blane had been so grumpy now. As an only child, she'd love a brother or sister to talk to.

'And you don't want to let him down, I guess,' was all she could offer.

'No, but what do I say?' asked Blane, getting worked up. '"I can't come and see you off cos I'm a teenage spy"?'

'Look,' cut in Rose determinedly. 'If we all work together, we can still crack this mission in time for you to see your brother. The Worm's too clever to get trapped online again, so our only option is to enter the Space Centre's computer system and defend it from attack.'

'Who'd do that?' asked Daisy, knowing it wasn't an area of expertise for any of them. 'You?'

'No, it's not my field,' admitted Rose. She had

no idea either. 'What we need is a gamer: someone with inside knowledge of the latest techniques.'

It didn't take them long to come up with a solution – Stewart!

'We rig his home computer to the launch program and tell him he's playing a missile-defence anti-hacking game!' decided Rose excitedly.

'But what if Stewart doesn't want to play?' Daisy questioned.

'He will,' grinned Blane, looking from Rose to Daisy and back again. 'If the right girl asks him.'

Rose looked at her feet as she got a weird butterfly feeling in her stomach. She could feel herself blushing. Stewart must like her! This could be her chance!

But when Rose looked up again, Blane wasn't looking at her. He was looking at Daisy.

'*Daisy?*' exclaimed Rose, unable to hide her dismay.

'Yeah, Stewart's . . .' started Blane, feeling slightly bad for revealing his best mate's secret.

'Stewart's what?' demanded Rose.

'He's got a bit of a thing for Daisy,' Blane admitted, not noticing Rose's fury. 'He thinks she looks like Queen Valhalla.'

'But she's a computer animation!' Rose was indignant. 'And anyway, why would someone clever like Stewart fancy Daisy?'

But Daisy's eyes were shining. It didn't surprise her that yet another boy fancied her. She was, after all, without a doubt, the coolest and cutest female within a hundred-mile radius.

Within minutes, Rose was hurrying along the corridor towards the lockers. She was trying to concentrate on the mission – Blane had given her his key to fetch a game they could overwrite. But she was still smarting from the fact that Stewart had taken a shine to Daisy and not her. The annoyingly chirpy voice of Ms Templeman coming up behind her did nothing to help her black mood.

'Have you finished the competition yet?' enquired her teacher brightly. Ms Templeman blinked at her expectantly.

Rose suddenly remembered the computer contest and grew flustered.

'Oh . . . no,' Rose stuttered, by way of reply. 'Not quite! But I'm working on it!'

Ms Templeman was taking another step towards her, looking worried. Her star pupil was certainly behaving very strangely.

'Are you OK, Rose?' she asked finally, her face etched with concern.

But Rose had turned and was hurrying off down the corridor. The last thing she needed was to be badgered about some stupid competition when the country could be on the verge of annihilation.

As she rushed past the classrooms, Rose could feel someone following her. Oh no – it was Ms Templeman!

Noticing she'd been spotted, the teacher stopped and pretended to look intensely interested in something out of the window.

With only a few metres separating them, Rose knelt down to fake doing up her shoelaces. She needed to buy herself a few seconds of time to think. Rose knew her and M.I. High's cover was under threat. She *had* to get away from her teacher. Suddenly, she remembered a technique from her training.

Straightening up, Rose sprinted to the open door of the next classroom along the corridor, leaned through the doorway and shouted at the top of her voice.

'Hey!' she yelled, 'Fifty Pence has got loads of those half-price DVDs!'

There was an immediate whooping as a long line of pupils poured out of the classroom, blocking Ms Templeman's path. Rose smiled. The promise of quality contraband was always guaranteed to pull an audience at St Hope's.

Without a minute to lose, Rose sped off down

the corridor to find Blane's locker. She didn't even have time to turn round as she heard a frustrated Ms Templeman calling out after her, hopelessly stuck in the swarm.

Chapter 7

The Worm purposefully tapped at his computer keys, a wicked smile spreading across his lips.

On the screen, The Worm could see the UK Space Centre Controller drenched in sweat, ripping off his tie and using it to mop up the rivers of perspiration gushing down his forehead. The tension in the Control Room would be *unbearable*. Squeaking with delight, he watched as the Controller stood silently in the middle of the room.

It was time for The Worm to turn.

He pressed a button on his keyboard with a gratifying jab and watched with satisfaction as the word 'HAZARD' flashed across every screen in the building. The Controller looked pale as he began typing furiously, referring to a file he'd already prepared beside his desk.

'Oh no!' The Worm heard the Controller cry with panic. 'It's that hacker again!'

The Worm scoffed. Only, the scoff sounded more like a childish giggle.

'Too easy!' he declared, licking his lips in front of the computer screen. 'Another wormhole in your security. Bet you can't wriggle out of this!'

Down in M.I. High HQ, Lenny answered the phone.

'Prime Minister,' he said, greeting the caller.

Daisy, Rose and Blane paid attention as the PM's voice came crackling through the handset.

'The Worm has hacked into the launch,' he informed Lenny. 'We can't wait any longer. I'm calling up the Fifth Commando Regiment.'

Blane's head felt like it was about to explode. That was Kyle's regiment! Daisy watched Blane with sympathy. He looked devastated.

'Please don't send in the troops, sir,' Lenny replied, genuinely concerned now that they were so close to finding a solution. 'We've established contact with the hacker and there're still forty-five minutes left to the deadline. My team has a plan in place.'

There was an agonizing pause as they listened to the PM sighing.

'Very well,' the teen spies heard him say curtly. 'But if you fail, they're going in.'

And with that the PM abruptly ended the call.

Daisy immediately grabbed the *Missile Defence*

CD that Blane had worked up to look like a real game and headed straight for the lift. There was no time to lose. As she quickly stepped inside, Daisy called out to Blane.

'I know – the Fifth Commando Regiment is your brother's unit,' she shouted, just as the doors began to close. 'I'll do my best, I promise!'

Even if that meant having to flirt with Stewart Critchley, Daisy said to herself ruefully as the lift hurtled upwards. The things a girl had to do to get by as a secret agent!

As Daisy soared towards ground level, the very distressed Controller was ending an important telephone call.

'The Prime Minister insists that we ignore the hacker for now,' the Controller said nervously, trying to sound authoritative. 'Commence initial countdown!'

After a frantic search, Daisy found Stewart hanging out forlornly by the school gates. He was still feeling pretty down about having no one to game against.

'Hey, Stew,' she said, skipping up to him with as much enthusiasm as her brilliant acting skills could muster. 'I hear you're looking for a partner to play *Queen Valhalla* with . . . so, um, your place?'

Daisy smiled winningly and twirled her hair around

43

her index finger. But inside she was cringing. What would happen to her trendsetter label if someone saw her and Stewart together?

Stewart, meanwhile, was flabbergasted. His Queen Valhalla, Daisy Millar, was actually talking to him. And not only that – she was inviting herself over to his place to play the greatest computer game on earth! Stewart looked to the heavens rapturously and sent up a silent thank you. This was a dream come true.

Just as Daisy was sure he was about to pick her up in his arms and carry her off to his house, Stewart's face dropped. A terrible thought had suddenly struck him.

'But I've got after-school stamp club!' he whimpered.

'I'm sure they won't miss you just this once,' Daisy reassured him, linking arms and leading Stewart out past the school gates. Secretly she was feeling a bit put out. Stewart was willing to miss having her, Daisy Millar, sit in his bedroom and play computer games for *stamp club*?

'I have this amazing new game called *Missile Defence*,' Daisy ploughed on, leading him down the road. 'It'll blow your mind!'

Stewart beamed at her. How could he really say no to this? Daisy Millar was so cool she'd managed to get hold of a new game he hadn't even heard of!

Slack-jawed and with their eyes the size of saucers, Zara and Kaleigh watched in disbelief as Daisy and Stewart headed off into the distance together. The two girls stood rooted to the spot.

Zara finally began stuttering in shock.

'Are you seeing what I'm seeing?' she asked, without breaking her stare.

Kaleigh nodded, pointing with a perfectly manicured nail to the side of her face. 'I think I need laser eye surgery!'

Neither of them wanted to believe it. It was enough trying to figure out why their super-gorgeous best friend was always hanging out with those weirdos Blane and Rose, but now she was wandering off with Stewart Critchley? What on earth was wrong with her?

Chapter 8

The fact that she was actually in Stewart Critchley's bedroom was enough to make any girl gross out. But instead, Daisy looked around for the computer. It wasn't hard to spot Stewart's prize possession. Daisy could easily see it sitting underneath a giant poster of Queen Valhalla and some loyal troll figurines on a desk in the corner.

'Any chance of a coffee?' Daisy asked sweetly, desperate to get Stewart out of the way while Rose helped her load up the program.

Stewart nodded dumbly and headed downstairs to put the kettle on. The moment he left the room, Daisy dashed over to the computer and inserted the *Missile Defence* CD.

'OK, Rose,' she whispered into her Pencil Communicator. 'Take me through the install while I try to keep him busy.'

In M.I. High HQ, Rose immediately began issuing instructions as Daisy's fingers flew over the keys. They were just getting into the swing of things when Daisy heard Stewart's footsteps approaching the bedroom.

'Er . . . sorry, Stew,' she sang, before he had a chance to open the door. 'I forgot to say, it's with two sugars.'

Stewart obediently turned round and went back downstairs. If it had been anyone else, he'd have told them to get the sugar themselves. But this was *Daisy Millar*!

Rose cracked on with the installation instructions and Daisy followed her commands to the letter. But they still weren't finished when Daisy heard Stewart reaching the top of the stairs again. She had to get rid of him!

'Um . . . it would be lovely with a biscuit,' she called out hopefully.

Stewart sighed and dutifully returned downstairs, but it wasn't long before the sound of Stewart's approaching feet was heard again. It hadn't taken him very long to find the biscuit box.

'Stew,' Daisy trilled, stopping him in his tracks outside the door. 'I like it with a lot of milk.'

Stewart shook his head in despair. Daisy was the cutest girl in the whole school, but his view of her was beginning to change. Once more he trooped down to the kitchen, wondering if even Queen Valhalla could be this demanding!

Meanwhile, up in Stewart's bedroom, the install was finally complete.

'You're hooked up to the launch program,' Rose said through Daisy's Pencil Communicator. 'The Worm's back in the mainframe. We need to get a trace on his PC as soon as possible.'

Rose finished her sentence just as Stewart staggered into the room with a downtrodden look on his face. Fulfilling Daisy's order had worn him out.

'That's one extra tall, double-shot, skinny, steamed decaf frappuccino,' he announced, plonking a coffee cup down on the desk. 'With two sugars and chocolate sprinkles.'

'Thanks, Stew, I do hope I'm no bother,' Daisy smiled, rewarding him with a sparkling grin. 'Anyway, now we're nice and cosy, let's play my new game – *Missile Defence*.'

As the game's opening credits flashed on-screen, Daisy was anxious to get Stewart started on saving the world.

'I've set it up for dual play, cos I want you to take on a friend of mine. He's a great player and has never lost a game. But I reckon you could beat him,' added Daisy, fluttering her eyelashes. 'If you do, I'll be *so* impressed.'

Stewart nodded eagerly. This sounded like his

kind of challenge! And he'd get to impress Daisy at the same time . . .

'OK,' he smiled, looking rather confident and pleased with himself. 'Prepare for some hot console action.'

'You're the Controller,' gushed Daisy, all too aware that time was running out. 'It's your job to launch a satellite that will make the UK safe from enemy attack.'

Stewart nodded. 'Bring 'em on!' he declared.

'My friend hacks into the system,' Daisy continued, pretending to be excited. 'He tries to stop the launch and blow it up. You have to defend the system and successfully complete the countdown.'

Stewart suddenly frowned.

'Hang on,' he said, holding up his hand. 'I think I'd rather be the hacker!'

'NO!' Daisy shouted hysterically. Realizing her mistake, Daisy lowered her voice and spoke more slowly. 'I mean no. The better player should always be the Controller. It's *much* more fun that way.'

'But it'd be cool to blow the satellite up,' Stewart pointed out, unconvinced by Daisy's argument.

'No, it wouldn't,' said Daisy firmly. 'Trust me!'

Stewart sighed. Daisy sure was a pushy gamer.

'OK, I guess we could always swap later,' he finally agreed, checking out the screen and spotting an icon that had just flashed up. 'Ooh, your friend's already online. "The Worm" – nice tag!'

As Daisy grappled with *Missile Defence*, down in M.I. High HQ Blane's feet were starting to get seriously itchy. He looked at the key-fob in his hand. The tracking device remained inactive.

'I think I've got time to see my brother before this trace activates,' he said hopefully to Rose.

Rose looked up at him uncertainly. She really wanted Blane to make the meeting, but he was the only one here to back her up. She couldn't do without him.

'Are you sure?' she said, knowing things could go wrong at any second. 'What if it locks on to The Worm?'

'Don't worry,' Blane promised, holding up his Pencil Communicator. 'The minute anything happens, I'll be straight on to it.'

Blane headed for the lift. He was the happiest he'd felt all day. He was going to see Kyle!

But before he could step inside, the Leyton Orient key-fob in his hands began to bleep. Blane turned round and caught Lenny's eye from across the other side of the room. He felt like the bottom of his world had just fallen out from underneath him.

'No way!' Blane muttered. This was the worst timing ever!

Chapter 9

'Oh, smart move!' cried Stewart at his computer screen. He was really getting into this *Missile Defence* game, but his anonymous competitor was pretty strong. 'The Worm's stopped me putting my fuel pump in place.'

'Well, come on!' trilled Daisy, her voice quivering. 'You've got to stop him doing that. You can stop him doing that, can't you?'

'Oh, I think so,' said Stewart cheerily, mistaking the desperation in her voice for enthusiasm. 'Swapping to override should do the trick.'

A drip of perspiration trickled across Daisy's perfectly made-up forehead and plopped down on to Stewart's keyboard. Daisy was mortified.

'Sorry!' she winced. 'I sweat when I'm nervous.'

'Oh!' Stewart smiled, hoping to reassure her. 'I get chesty under pressure.'

Ewww . . . disgusting. Daisy eyed the screen anxiously. Stewart wasn't doing as well as she'd hoped. Didn't he realize Britain's future was under threat? Daisy sighed. Of course he didn't.

'Keep concentrating,' Daisy commanded. 'Go to the next level.'

'Check, I'm removing the launch gantry and clearing ground personnel . . .' Stewart stared at the screen in amazement. 'Wow! Those CGI men are so realistic!'

That's because they ARE real, thought Daisy.

The excitement was getting a bit too much for Stewart to handle. He stood up abruptly.

'I need my inhaler,' he announced, ambling out of the room to find it.

'But what about the launch?' Daisy shouted frantically after Stewart.

The lift doors were beginning to slide shut on Blane. He'd decided he didn't care if the dumb tracking device was flashing. He was going to see his brother.

But any excitement Blane might have felt came to a sudden halt as a hand abruptly pressed against one of the doors and held it open. It was Lenny.

'I'd really like to help intercept The Worm,' explained Blane firmly, 'but my brother comes first. I have to go and see him.'

'To warn him not to join the regiment?' asked Lenny icily.

'Look, we've done all we can with this missile defence thing,' Blane replied, anger rising in his voice.

'It can still stop the war and take The Worm out of the equation for good,' Lenny replied calmly.

'But what if we can't?' asked Blane. 'This is for real. Stewart thinks he's playing a stupid game, but there're no second chances and no extra lives. If he fails, it's game over, and it'll be my brother in the firing line.'

'It's a big sacrifice,' Lenny conceded, 'but putting the lives of others before our loved ones is what we do. Believe me, I've been there.'

Blane looked at the flashing key-fob in his hand. He hated to admit it, but Lenny was right. He had to trace The Worm first.

As it turned out, The Worm's trail of havoc was starting to grow bigger by the second. With Stewart out of the room, Daisy watched in horror as warning lights started flashing across the control panel on-screen.

In the Space Centre, the Controller was sporting much the same look.

'It's just like last time!' he screamed. 'Prepare to abort launch!'

Daisy's shrieking brought Stewart rushing back into the room, hurriedly taking a couple of puffs from his inhaler.

53

'Do something!' Daisy bawled. 'We're losing!'

Stewart calmly sat back down next to Daisy. For someone so cool, she was starting to embarrass herself. Stewart tutted to himself. If Daisy was going to learn to be a good gamer, she really needed to just get a grip.

'I did learn this game tip off a blog site once,' he said, watching the lights as they continued to flash manically on the screen. 'It worked on *Queen Valhalla*. Basically, you fake defeat.'

'Isn't that risky?' asked Daisy, her voice rising.

'Er . . . yes,' agreed Stewart, quickly pressing a couple of keys. 'But it's all we've got!'

Daisy closed her eyes and hoped that Stewart's strategy would come good. If it didn't, then . . . well, it just had to!

'There he is!' laughed Stewart victoriously, pointing at the screen in delight. 'He's fallen for it! Anti-viral killerbots in action!'

On the screen a series of blue mini-robots advanced towards the worm icon, firing deathly rays. Daisy held her breath. The worm icon flickered several times and then vanished. Completely.

The word 'DESTROYED' flashed across the screen.

'Way to go!' yelled Stewart triumphantly, punching

the air as Daisy looked like she was about to faint. 'Now if we're lucky . . . resuming countdown!'

In the Space Centre, the Controller was feeling much the same. Under the PM's orders, he still had to continue with the launch, whatever the consequence.

'Resuming countdown,' he announced hoarsely.

Once again, the automated voice immediately kicked off.

'Nine . . . eight . . . seven . . . six . . .'

'No sign of an intruder,' the Controller whispered to no one in particular, shaking with nerves.

'Five . . . four . . . three . . . two . . .'

The Controller covered his eyes.

'One,' the voice finished.

In the Space Centre, M.I. High HQ and even Stewart's bedroom, everyone held their breath.

'LAUNCH!'

The Controller took his hands away from his eyes and watched the fiery blast of the rocket's engines on-screen as it soared safely upwards into the sky.

The Control Room went crazy. Cheering, screaming and high-fiving filled the building as the Controller began to shout.

'Get the sponge cake out, guys!' he yelled triumphantly, sweat cascading off his body in torrents. 'It's party time!'

Chapter 10

'Yay, yay!' screamed Daisy, leaping around Stewart's bedroom like a maniac. She couldn't believe it. The Worm had been defeated! The country was safe again!

Daisy threw her arms round Stewart and gave him an embarrassingly tight hug. For once, she didn't care. She could have hugged anyone after surviving that super-close call. Even dorky Stewart Critchley!

'Steady on!' Stewart said, trying to push her away. Daisy's over-the-top behaviour was seriously weirding him out. 'It's just a game.'

But Daisy continued her celebrations, jumping around his bedroom. Each little pogo bounce was peppered with chants of 'We did it! We did it!'

Stewart took a deep puff from his inhaler. He needed to tell Daisy something pretty heavy and now was as good a time as any to get it over and done with.

'Er . . . today's been great,' said Stewart, as he

approached Daisy nervously. 'And I really enjoyed playing *Missile Defence* with your friend . . .'

'Yeah?' cut in Daisy, about to take off for another lap of the room.

'But . . . er,' Stewart searched for the right words. 'There's no easy way to put this . . . I'm not ready for a relationship. We're finished.'

Daisy's grin instantly disappeared.

'Huh? You're dumping me?' she asked incredulously. That's not how it was supposed to happen!

Stewart put a reassuring hand on her shoulder.

'You and me . . . it'll never work,' he said, registering her jaw drop and assuming it was just disappointment. 'I'm sure you'll find someone else one day.'

A stunned Daisy was left speechless. Dumped by Stewart Critchley when you hadn't even been going out with him. How low could a girl get?

While this touching scene was playing out in Stewart's bedroom, his defeated opponent held his head in his hands. The Worm couldn't understand how his dastardly plot had been foiled.

The Worm sensed someone appear in the doorway of his room. But he was too upset to talk to anyone now.

'Not now, Mummy,' The Worm said irritably, with his back to the door. 'I'm busy.'

But the person didn't budge. The Worm was getting annoyed. Why couldn't his mum just leave him alone?

The Worm spun round furiously and came face-to-face . . . with Blane.

'Who are you?' The Worm asked, sticking his nose up in the air.

'Just as Daisy predicted,' declared Blane, scowling at the pathetic-looking schoolkid sitting in front of him, wearing a green jumper and studious specs. This was the reason he was missing out on seeing Kyle? Some stupid kid running a hacking operation from his bedroom!

'You're under arrest for hacking into the SPARTA launch.'

But the kid wasn't finished yet. He'd show them how powerful The Worm could still be! Grabbing a toy sucker gun, he fired an orange dart at Blane. The M.I.9 agent leapt out of the way, just as the dart went careering past him.

'Those amateurs!' snorted the cyber-hacker, continuing his assault. 'Please don't make The Worm laugh!'

The kid fired another dart at Blane but the spy ducked just in time. Who did this dweeb think he was? Blane grabbed an inflatable space rocket off the floor and aimed it at his attacker's head. The kid fell to the floor, but in an instant picked up another inflatable rocket and began hitting back.

'This isn't some dumb kids' game,' shouted Blane as they traded blows. 'Your stupid pranks nearly sent us to war!'

Blane could see the dart gun out of the corner of his eye. Snatching it up, he fired an orange dart smack bang into one of the lenses of the schoolkid's glasses.

The skinny boy staggered backwards but managed to recover before falling over.

'Wise up, worm boy!' commanded Blane. 'National security isn't just rockets and computers. It's real people: life and death.'

He was furious now. Blane gave the dart gun another go. This time, the dart connected perfectly with the other lens of The Worm's spectacles. The boy fell backwards on to his bed as Blane continued his verbal assault.

'My brother could have died because of your pathetic games!' he snarled, grabbing a green alien mask from high on a shelf and shoving it over the kid's head. He lifted the pathetic figure up by the back of his jacket.

Just then, a kind-looking woman appeared in the

doorway. She was holding two glasses of orange juice and didn't appear to notice that she had one of Britain's most wanted cyber-criminals and an M.I.9 agent in her house.

'I don't know what you boys do in here all day,' she said with an affectionate smile.

'Computer club fancy-dress party,' explained Blane innocently, leading the green-masked kid past her. 'Sorry.'

'Er . . . bye, Mummy,' came a muffled voice from under the alien mask. This was going to be the one game The Worm couldn't hack his way out of.

Chapter 11

Lenny was delighted. Despite a few hiccups, his M.I.9 protégés had successfully thwarted The Worm hacker. Together!

'Well done,' he beamed, turning to Blane. 'Doing the right thing usually brings its own rewards.'

'Maybe you should get to the railway station,' Rose suggested to her fellow agent hopefully.

Blane shook his head. 'What's the point? I'm way too late.'

'Surely it's worth a try?' said Lenny softly, a world away from his harsh stance earlier in the day. 'There might have been delays: leaves on the line, or even a shortage of teabags at Crewe.'

Blane managed a weak smile at Lenny's joke. He might be right – he *might* just make it! He took off towards the lift.

Lenny looked over at the small pathetic figure cowering in a chair. The alien mask made it seem like some kind of mini-martian.

'Now what about our friend The Worm?' Lenny mused.

'The Worm's been really stupid,' spluttered the muffled voice inside the mask. 'He can see that now.'

He went to stand up, but Daisy and Rose quickly shoved him back down.

'He might be useful on our side,' said Lenny thoughtfully. 'Once we've re-educated him.'

But Rose wasn't wondering about the future of the cyber-hacker any more. She had something more important on her mind.

'I don't suppose Stewart mentioned me at all, did he?' she asked Daisy, trying with some success to sound completely casual.

Rose trudged out of the storeroom, walking sadly through the main corridor of St Hope's. Daisy's silence had crushed any hope she might have had that Stewart actually liked her. Just because she didn't look like stupid Queen Valhalla!

As Rose headed towards her locker, she once again ran into Ms Templeman.

'Ah, Rose,' called her form tutor. *What a relief*. She'd had enough of looking in the ladies' for Rose all afternoon. 'The computer competition?'

Rose looked blank for a second and then quickly reached among her papers and pulled out the sheet about the contest. She hadn't even had a chance to look at it! Rose ran her eyes over the information and did a quick bit of mental calculation.

'Er . . . the answer to the maths puzzle,' she said, numbers racing through her head, 'is . . . er . . . twenty-nine!'

'Mr Briley from the maths department made it minus nought point seven,' Ms Templeman replied, frowning. 'We thought that must be wrong!'

Rose tried to walk off, but Ms Templeman hadn't quite finished with her.

'And the slogan?' she asked expectantly.

The slogan? Rose hadn't even known about a slogan! 'Er . . . your school day will be ready for lift-off with Intral Computers,' she volunteered.

'Rose, that's wonderful!' Ms Templeman gushed. 'I knew you'd come through. I hope you didn't spend all day on it.'

Ms Templeman smiled brightly as she watched Rose walk away and thought of all the wonderful computers they were going to win. So what if Rose had been acting a little strangely lately? She was still the smartest pupil in the whole of St Hope's!

Blane was trudging back to school. He'd missed Kyle by a long shot and was feeling really miserable. He wouldn't see Kyle again for weeks.

Just then, however, he spotted a khaki-clad figure standing with his back to him at the school gates. His heart began to thump with anticipation.

'Kyle?' whispered Blane incredulously.

The khaki figure turned round and Blane's heart leapt. It was his big brother all right! Blane felt like he might burst into tears on the spot.

'Where the heck were you?' Kyle asked, giving him a good-natured punch on the arm. 'Good job my call-up got cancelled at the last minute!'

Kyle put his arm round his younger brother's shoulders as they started walking home together. Blane was beaming . . . all the mission work had been worth it. If only he'd realized that stopping The Worm meant that Kyle wouldn't have to go off again, he might not have caused so many headaches for everybody – including himself!

'You all right?' grinned Kyle. 'What you been up to?'

Blane fixed his brother a modest grin as he thought back over the incredible events of the day.

'Nothing much!' came the reply.

Two weeks later, Mr Flatley stood outside a classroom door, grinning with delight. Ms Templeman was standing faithfully at his side, pretending to be fascinated by another of her Headmaster's famously boring speeches.

Several kids were yawning openly. Mr Flatley ignored them.

'. . . So it is with great pleasure,' the Headmaster said, finally wrapping up his speech, 'that I declare the new computer suite open.'

The St Hope's Headmaster then turned round and threw open the computer suite door dramatically. But the wide smile on his face was immediately swept away as a startling sight greeted him.

On each table was a keyboard and mouse but no . . . actual computers. A curtain by the open window flapped idly in the breeze.

'Stolen . . . *already*?' gasped Mr Flatley, turning desperately to Ms Templeman. Why did nothing last five minutes at St Hope's? Mr Flatley let his shoulders drop, already admitting defeat.

'Not even M.I.9 could protect this place!' he said sadly.

Daisy, Rose and Blane couldn't stop themselves from bursting into laughter. If only poor Mr Flatley knew the truth!

The Fugitive

Chapter 1

It was early morning as Stewart Critchley ambled up a quiet residential street on his way to another boring day of school at St Hope's. His mind definitely wasn't on school, though. Like most days, he was thinking about his latest computer game. This time, it was a particularly stubborn dragon blocking his path on Level 22. Stewart frowned and scratched his scruffy blond hair. Maybe his best mate, Blane, would know how to get around it.

As Stewart started to cross the street, a huge eerie sound filled the skies. He went to put his hands over his ears – he'd heard nothing this loud outside a multiplex cinema!

Glancing upwards, Stewart's hands froze in mid-air. Right above him, flitting across the sky, was a large, round metallic object. His eyes widened as he watched the mystery craft dip behind a row of houses and disappear. A large plume of grey smoke began to drift up into the air. Stewart gaped in wonder.

This could be his lucky day!

After *years* of trying to convince Blane that aliens were regularly landing on Earth and secretly communicating with the British government, Stewart would *finally* be able to get proof. All he had to do was locate the crashed UFO and take a photo.

He could hardly believe it. He'd picked up alien communications on an old makeshift radio once, but that was nothing compared to *this*. So much for another boring day at school!

It was the last lesson of the day and the Year Nine teacher Ms Templeman was droning on about the finer points of protozoa, not that anyone at the back of the class was listening. Even after listening to Stewart recount his UFO encounter for the umpteenth time, Blane still felt sceptical. He was used to Stewart's 'evidence' on the existence of aliens and none of it ever amounted to anything.

But Stewart remained undeterred. 'You do realize, when we find the wreckage, we'll be, like, *heroes* of the UFO community.'

'*We?*' Blane repeated, raising an eyebrow at his mate. Stewart was on another planet if he thought

Blane wanted to join him on the front cover of *Conspiracy Nuts* magazine.

'More conspiracy theories, boys?'

Rose Gupta eyed them with a smirk. She loved science and was listening to Ms Templeman as intently as ever, but as she was sitting on the opposite side of their table it had been impossible for her not to overhear the boys' conversation.

'What's it this time? Little green men?' Rose teased. She liked Stewart, but he could be seriously *weird* sometimes.

By now the argument had also attracted the interest of Daisy Millar, who sauntered over to the table to find out what all the fuss was about. Daisy was St Hope's one it-girl and could turn boys to mush just by *looking* at them. But Stewart was in no mood to swoon today.

'UFOs exist,' he was insisting, 'and I'm gonna prove it.'

Ms Templeman looked on as the scene played out and sighed. She was conscious that despite the lesson being nearly over, hardly any of her pupils had actually completed their work. To Ms Templeman, teaching sometimes felt like a never-ending treadmill and today she felt she'd done more miles than a hamster training for the marathon.

'Right, back to your groups,' she declared, jangling

the colourful bracelets on her arms as she tried to gesture authoritatively. 'The bell hasn't rung yet!'

Daisy sloped back to her desk. Even though he was the biggest nerd she knew, aside from Rose, Daisy had been enjoying Stewart's mad ranting. At least it was more interesting than science class.

Putting her marking aside, Ms Templeman began wandering around the class until her eyes came to rest on a fascinating object sitting in front of her star pupil, Rose Gupta. It looked like a fat bicycle pump with a translucent section in the middle.

'Well, Rose,' she said, with obvious admiration, 'this looks *very* impressive.'

'It's a dimensional stabilizer, Miss,' Rose explained, turning it over in her hands. 'It can maintain an object's tensile strength, even at extreme velocity.'

Ms Templeman nodded, pretending that she understood what Rose had just told her. But secretly she was fascinated. Rose was a real scientific genius and the whatever-it-was *must* be good for something. Ms Templeman lifted up the invention for the rest of the class to see.

'A stabilizing . . . thing!' she told them, adding a dramatic sweep with her hand. 'Why can't the rest of you be a little more like Rose?'

The entire class looked at Rose blankly until she could feel her face starting to burn. She couldn't understand the fuss – it was only a dimension stabilizer, after all!

Rose's humiliation only ended when the bell rang for home time.

'You *are* coming to look for this UFO, right?' Stewart asked Blane as they picked up their things and headed for the door.

But before Blane could answer, a familiar light started buzzing from the end of the pencil he was holding. Blane quickly covered the Pencil Communicator with his jumper and hoped Stewart hadn't noticed.

'Er, actually . . .' he hesitated, trying to think of an excuse. But clocking the faraway look on his friend's face, it was obvious Stewart was too busy thinking about aliens to notice the light at all. *Just as well.* Blane left him to it and took off down the corridor. He had to find Daisy and Rose.

A very excited Stewart barely registered Blane had gone. He was imagining thousands of adoring sci-fi fans chanting his name. He, Stewart Critchley, was going to nail some proof of UFO existence once and for all!

Chapter 2

Blane rendezvoused with a bright-eyed Rose and Daisy at the entrance to the M.I. High lift. Lenny had also summoned them on their Pencil Communicators and they were hoping it was time for a new mission.

As they emerged through the doors at the bottom of the lift, their school uniforms had been replaced by their black agent spywear. Now out of his shabby caretaker outfit and decked out in his smart purple suit, Lenny looked satisfactorily at the three young agents lining up before him. It had been months since he had personally selected Daisy, Rose and Blane from the students of St Hope's, trained them and become their mentor. After several successful missions, he felt certain they were already among the finest agents in the country.

But this was no time for pleasantries.

'An unmanned space probe has crashed in the vicinity of this school,' Lenny said seriously.

Down in the M.I. High headquarters, Lenny was
waiting to brief his agents.

Rose admitted they'd blown their only lead.

'The Prime Minister wants an update!'

Blane was determined. It was time to unearth The Worm.

The control room erupted into cheers. Britain was safe!

Was Lenny still on their side?

It was the first time Lenny had seen his former protégée Carla Terrini for many years.

Lenny was puzzled. The agents were nowhere to be seen.

Realizing how upset Blane was about missing his brother,
Daisy wished she could help.

Unfortunately, Agents 1 and 2 just weren't
the sharpest tools in the box.

'Maybe one day we meet at a science conference!'
Lu suggested hopefully to Rose.

M.I. High bid their new friend, Lu, farewell.

Stewart's suggestion that they were spies
was totally ridiculous!

'Wow!' Blane was impressed. 'Stewart was right about those aliens!'

'Not exactly,' cautioned Lenny. 'The probe was launched by a hostile foreign power. It's your job to search for the wreckage and, if you find it, to secure the site until Air One arrive.'

'Who are Air One?' asked Rose, confused.

Blane shook his head with disbelief. How could Rose not know *that*?

'Air One are, like, this legendary special unit,' he explained patiently. 'They deal with anything weird or unidentified entering UK air space.'

However, Rose wasn't convinced. 'I don't see why *we* couldn't just handle it *ourselves*,' she said sulkily. She liked to think that M.I. High could solve everything on their own.

Lenny smiled.

'I like the confidence, Rose,' he said, 'but Air One want to study the craft technology and they have jurisdiction over M.I.9. Besides, Carla heads up a great team.'

'Who's this Carla?' asked Daisy, always wary of any female competition. Lenny certainly hadn't mentioned *Carla* during training.

'Carla Terrini,' Lenny replied, his eyes slightly misting over. 'She won the Young Spy of the Year Award five times in a row. Ring any bells?'

His three agents looked back at him blankly.

'Ah, no, of course not.' Lenny nodded thoughtfully. 'The contest's pretty hush-hush.'

'Why didn't *I* get entered?' Daisy whined, sounding a little petulant.

'The entry forms are in invisible ink,' replied Lenny, by way of explanation. 'So it's not easy.'

Daisy scowled at him. *What a lame excuse!* If she'd been put forward, there was no doubt she would have won it. Didn't Lenny think they were good enough to enter a stupid spy competition?

'Anyway,' Lenny continued, ignoring Daisy's dirty look and picking up a stack of traffic-cone-like objects from the floor, 'Carla wants us to secure the site using these pods.'

The pods looked ordinary enough, but Lenny explained they emitted a powerful but invisible force field.

'Cool,' Daisy observed drily. 'Maybe I can use them to deter boys.'

'Believe me,' Blane laughed, 'you don't need a pod to do that!'

Daisy threw Blane a scathing look. *As if!* She was the prettiest girl in school and he knew it! She held a perfectly manicured hand up to her head and flipped her long blonde hair back so he could see her perfect profile.

Lenny didn't have time for squabbling and handed his agents two pods each.

'Blane, you take the area out the back of school,' he instructed. 'Daisy and Rose – check out the surrounding neighbourhood.'

Obediently clutching the pods to their chests, the three teenage spies hurried for the lift as Lenny turned towards a workstation. But just as the doors were about to close, Rose spotted an extra pod on the floor.

'Who's going back for the last one?' she asked.

Daisy and Blane looked at her pointedly. Rose sighed. Why was she always the one who had to pick up the pieces?

Rose stepped out of the lift. But before she reached the cone Rose heard the noise of a tape spooling backwards and a curt voice.

With his back turned to her, Lenny had inserted a pencil into a large grey pencil sharpener. He wasn't aware of Rose's presence as he listened to the message:

This is an ears-only communiqué. Project ASD3 must be transferred for examination immediately. This communiqué will self-destruct in five seconds.

Lenny seemed to tense up as he sensed a presence behind him. He spun round and came face-to-face with Rose.

'Um . . . just testing some new hardware,' he stuttered, looking oddly uncomfortable.

Rose eyed him suspiciously. She had never seen Lenny like that before. He always seemed so together – so on top of things. Yet here he was, looking like some guilty little schoolboy.

'I need the last pod,' Rose said, looking at him carefully.

'Oh, of course, yes,' nodded Lenny, his eye twitching. He quickly picked up the remaining cone and handed it to her.

A sudden hissing noise came from the pencil sharpener as the pencil was incinerated in a whirring cloud of smoke.

'Back to the drawing board, I suppose,' Lenny laughed nervously, giving her a weak smile.

He watched as Rose frowned and walked back towards the lift. Lenny hoped he had managed to convince her. The last thing he wanted was the team asking awkward questions, today of all days . . .

Meanwhile, at the bus stop near St Hope's, a young man named Colin was hungrily devouring a tub of noodles. Although he was chowing down as if he hadn't eaten for a week, it wasn't like he was in a particular hurry today. In fact, Colin wasn't in a particular hurry any day.

That was because he was the kind of student who prided himself on spending as little time as possible at college, where he was currently undertaking a sandwich course in archaeology. Instead, he preferred to while away the hours in the cinema or wandering across London with his beloved metal detector, in search of undiscovered treasure. But the closest he'd ever come to that was finding twenty pence left in the coin-return chute of a BT phone box.

Colin's mobile sounded. He swallowed his noodles with a gulp as a smooth, plummy and very familiar voice greeted him.

'Hi, Uncle . . . er . . . Grand Master,' Colin answered uncertainly. Hearing that voice always slightly unnerved him. 'What's up?'

'What's up,' replied the voice, mimicking Colin sarcastically, 'is that a mysterious, super-fast space pod has crashed in your vicinity. General Flopsy and I think that such technology would be well worth acquiring.'

Colin groaned. He'd heard his uncle talk like this before. Colin thought he was a bit of an eccentric. He could just imagine his uncle now, sitting in a darkened room with his pet rabbit General Flopsy on his lap.

'You're not trying to take over the world again, are you?' Colin asked warily.

'If I was, you'd be the last person I'd tell,' the icy voice replied.

'Yeah, that's cos it'll never happen,' muttered Colin, half to himself. 'So how come you want me to find this space probe thingy?'

There was a slight pause at the other end of the line. 'All my best agents have been poached by a competitor.'

'But it's half price for students at Cinema World this afternoon!' Colin cried. He never missed the half-price show – it was *such* good value for money!

On the other end of the line, the Grand Master's patience was being severely stretched. How on earth had he, a sinister criminal genius, ended up with a nephew as dense as Colin?

'This is a big carrot the General and I are dangling,' he hissed down the phone. 'It's the chance to impress us and become a permanent S.K.U.L. agent!'

Back at the bus stop, Colin thought hard. He'd never really understood what kind of business his uncle ran, but if he could get a cushy job instead of having to go through college, it might just be worth it.

'Oh, all right,' Colin replied, suddenly looking forward to the giant box of popcorn. 'I'll get on to it when I've finished me noodles.'

Chapter 3

Air One had swiftly moved in and set up their base on a field sitting behind St Hope's School. A large blue trailer was parked alongside two open tents containing tables, chairs and technical equipment.

Two Air One agents were already patrolling the site. Anyone watching them from a distance would have believed them to be highly skilled security operatives. But the truth of the matter was that these two particular agents had only recently just scraped through their training.

Agent 1 stood with his feet parted, bitterly complaining to Agent 2. Both were wearing ridiculously restrictive leather uniforms and oversized hi-tech sunglasses.

'It's hard to look cool when your trousers are so tight!' he protested, tugging in frustration at the material on his hips.

Agent 2 looked at him and nodded in solace. Not only were his trousers cutting into his inner thigh, they were at least three millimetres too short. He looked mournfully across the nondescript field. If only he were back in Ibiza.

The two agents continued their separate patrols as Lenny, now dressed in a smart mac, strolled towards the Air One trailer. A beautiful woman, with intense brown eyes and dark hair scraped back off her face, walked down the stairs to greet him. Her stride was so smooth and precise that if you hadn't known she was human, you might have wondered if she wasn't some sort of gorgeous android.

'Carla!' Lenny called, greeting his former protégée with a warm smile. She was just as stunning as he remembered. 'Or should I say "Ma'am"?'

'So this is home now,' nodded Carla coolly, indicating the school in the distance. 'It's been too long.'

'It's hard to keep up now you're such a high-flyer,' Lenny beamed. It was so good to finally see Carla again. 'I was so proud.'

'I owe it all to you. Let's not forget that.' Carla fixed him with a stare and lowered her voice conspiratorially. 'How's the hip?'

'Fine,' grinned Lenny. 'But I think my days of chasing enemy agents down Mont Blanc are over.'

Carla's steady gaze twitched in an almost-smile as Lenny took her back to those seemingly carefree days. But her face froze when the two patrolling agents passed in front of them.

'So how's my hair, is it OK?' Agent 1 was fussing to Agent 2, waving his hands around his head. 'More gel, less gel?'

Carla's eyes narrowed.

'You've either got it or you haven't,' she observed to Lenny, indicating her agents with a disapprovingly raised eyebrow. 'And those two definitely haven't!'

'Oh, mud! I hate mud,' Daisy moaned. 'Mud is for boys and pigs.'

'Is there a difference?' asked Rose, a few steps ahead, as the two girls carefully picked their way along a track.

The secret agents were out in St Hope's Park on the trail of the space probe. So far, pushing through hedges and inspecting ponds, they'd found no sign of it. But their luck was about to change.

'Hey, Daisy!' Rose yelled. 'I think I've found something!'

Daisy pelted after her friend. Hidden behind some foliage in a clearing was a circle of singed black grass.

'Look at these scorch marks,' said Rose enthusiastically, crouching down for a closer look. 'It must be the retro-rockets slowing her down.'

Reaching out for some blackened leaves hanging

off a branch, Daisy studied the scene. It looked as though the probe had bounced and hit a tree. So it just *had* to be nearby!

As Daisy and Rose continued moving through the thicket, another figure on the other side of the park was becoming equally excited.

As his metal detector beeped wildly, Colin was jumping on the spot.

'The probe!' he cried eagerly. Colin dropped the machine and grabbed a white oval object off the ground.

Lifting it delicately in his hands, Colin couldn't help letting out a whistle of admiration as he ran his hands over the smooth surface. It looked like the rim of something important. *It was beautiful!*

'A window from the cockpit,' he murmured in awe. 'Made from some hi-tech carbon.'

Colin held the oval up to his face and peered through, picturing far-off galaxies. But his daydream was interrupted by a loud voice behind him.

'It's a *toilet* seat,' said the voice, sending Colin jolting backwards in fright to land in a large patch of stinging nettles. A thin, gangly silhouette towered over him as he squinted back up into the sunlight. Colin's mind raced. *Was it one of the aliens coming to claim him?*

Stewart held out his hand. Only when he finally realized that the figure was just a skinny schoolkid did Colin grab it gratefully.

'I need a dock leaf,' Colin proclaimed, scratching his arm. 'It's an old secret-agent trick for falling in nettles.'

'You're a secret agent?' Stewart gasped, his face lighting up. 'What are you doing round here?'

Colin eyed the kid cautiously. What did his uncle always say about looks being deceptive?

'Er . . . I'm . . . just looking for artefacts,' he replied. 'Car boot sale on Saturday. You?'

'Well, I'm on the trail of a UFO,' Stewart said proudly.

A look of relief swept across Colin's face. This kid wasn't one of the enemy after all. He must work for S.K.U.L. too! And he could really use some help.

'Oh, you're on the space-probe thingy as well!' Colin cheered, clapping his hands. 'Why didn't you say? My name's Agent Zero, er, Colin.'

Stewart couldn't believe his luck. *A real-life agent!* If Blane didn't want to look for extraterrestrials with him, it didn't matter. Stewart had a real-life secret agent to help him now. He and Colin shook hands, delighted in their new understanding. They were a probe-hunting team!

Chapter 4

It wasn't long before Daisy and Rose found what they were looking for. There in the clearing in front of them was the circular space probe, measuring about four metres in diameter. Its peculiar metallic silver casing was topped by a glass dome. The craft looked badly damaged.

Without saying a word, Daisy whipped out her Pencil Communicator.

'Lenny!' she shouted, squealing in delight. 'We've found the probe!'

'Is it all right if I take a look?' Rose asked, grabbing the Communicator from Daisy. 'It's not what I expected. It's *incredible*!'

'No, I'm sorry, Rose,' came Lenny's stern reply. 'Position the pods and activate the force field. Then wait till Air One arrive.'

Rose pursed her lips unhappily and signed off.

'I don't know why,' she said to Daisy, 'but I feel

like we're being sidelined.' She was *sure* something else was going on with Lenny.

But Daisy was too excited by their discovery to worry about Lenny. She snatched the Pencil Communicator back and immediately made contact with Blane.

'Blane, we've found the probe,' she announced in a particularly superior tone, 'so you can stop looking now.'

'Very clever,' replied Blane, refusing to rise to the bait. 'But you haven't found everything. I'm at the gym and you both need to get here *now*.'

Daisy and Rose frowned at each other, startled. *What else was there to look for?* Still, an essential part of their job as secret agents was to back each other up. Even though Lenny had told them to stay until Air One arrived, it was doubtful anyone else was looking for the probe. Surely it would be OK to help Blane and return as soon as they could? They headed back towards the school.

The two girls found Blane waiting in St Hope's down-at-heel gym. They arrived out of breath and looking rather annoyed to find nothing out of the ordinary – it was the same old bleak gym. Battered wooden horse vaults were set out on the floor along with shabby green mats.

'This'd better be good,' Daisy said irritably. 'We're supposed to be guarding the crash site.'

Without saying a word, Blane looked down at the gym floor and pointed at a trail of slimy green footprints.

'Eww!' frowned Daisy, disgusted. 'Looks like something out of Fifty Pence's nose.'

Rose knelt down and dipped her finger in the substance. She held it up to her nose as Daisy gagged.

'It smells like petrol,' Rose observed thoughtfully. 'It's all around the probe too.'

Her train of thought was interrupted as Daisy held her finger up to her lips.

'Ssshh,' she commanded. 'I think I heard something!'

They listened for a moment. *There it was again!* The teen spies could all hear a very slight creaking sound. Fear spread over Daisy's face.

'OK, this is getting freaky,' she whispered. 'We'd better call Lenny.'

Rose wasn't so sure. She worried that Lenny didn't have their best interests at heart on this mission. His behaviour at headquarters this morning had seriously weirded her out.

But at that second all three of the team heard the creaking noise again. This time it was obvious – and it was coming from an old wooden box used to store sports equipment on the other side of the gym!

The teen agents didn't stick around. They dived for cover behind a nearby horse vault and carefully peered out over the top.

They then watched with baited breath as the lid of the box slowly began to open. A loud thud echoed around the gym as the lid clattered to the floor. To their utter amazement, a tiny figure began to emerge. And to their relief the alien had two arms and two legs like them. But it also wore a weird full-face helmet that hid its features, and which seemed to be made from an unfamiliar shiny black material. It was like nothing they'd ever seen before! The 'alien' climbed slowly out of the box and alighted silently on to the floor of the gym. It was unaware of their presence.

'Looks like the space probe had a pilot after all,' whispered Blane, hardly able to get the words out.

'Yeah,' added Daisy. 'Some *freaky* alien. Let's get out of here!'

But just as she was about to bolt for the door, Blane and Rose pulled her down again. They couldn't just leave an extraterrestrial wandering around St Hope's.

They'd have to sort this out by themselves . . .

M.I.HIGH

Chapter 5

Over in St Hope's Park, Carla Terrini was white with fury. Air One had just managed to track down the space probe, surrounded by the pods. But Blane, Daisy and Rose were nowhere in sight. They appeared to have deserted their post.

'So where is your team?' Carla glared angrily at Lenny. 'I can't believe they've left the site unmanned.' There was little sign of the friendship they'd displayed towards each other earlier.

'There must be a simple explanation,' soothed Lenny. It wasn't like Daisy and Rose to disappear completely, but he had to give them the benefit of the doubt.

It looked like Carla was refusing to be placated. She didn't have time for excuses – Carla Terrini hadn't been Young Spy of the Year five times running for nothing.

'We need to find out where they are,' Carla demanded, barking orders. 'Activate the transponders; we'll track their Pencil Communicators.'

Lenny was shocked. Tracking an agent's Communicator was the ultimate betrayal of trust, but he had no choice. He reached into his coat pocket and reluctantly pulled out a silver unit, resembling an incredibly smart, new-generation mobile phone. A red light flashed on its panel as it instantly started to trace his team.

Rose stood up silently from behind the horse vault and began walking bravely towards the figure, which by now was standing motionless in the middle of the gym. Although they wouldn't admit it, Daisy and Blane were relieved that Rose had volunteered. Both were frightened about how the alien would react to human contact.

'This is a classic first-encounter scenario,' Rose reminded the team. 'We need to defuse the situation and determine identity via initial information exchange.'

'Huh?' Blane hissed to Daisy. Was she speaking some crazy alien language already or what?

'She's spouting from the spy manual again,' explained Daisy, rolling her eyes.

Trying not to show how terrified she really was, Rose slowly drew closer to the alien . . .

'Do. You. Speak. English?' she asked.

The alien cocked its head and looked at her quizzically. It didn't seem to understand.

'How about we try using a simple binary code?' she suggested.

Rose pulled out her mobile phone, tapping in a sequence of numbers and passed the phone to the alien. It took the contraption in its black-gloved hand, hit several keys and passed the mobile back to her.

A big grin appeared on Rose's face.

'He says he comes in peace!' she called excitedly to Daisy and Blane, who were still behind the horse vault.

But before they could find out any more about the mystery spaceman, Blane glimpsed two men that looked like Air One agents running through the schoolyard outside the gym windows. The shorter one in tight leather trousers was holding a silver gadget out in front of him.

'Air One!' Blane shouted.

'Lenny must have given them the transponder unit,' said Rose, recognizing the silver device. She was now one-hundred-percent certain that Lenny was in league with Carla over *something*.

Signalling to Blane, Daisy and Rose grabbed the startled alien-pilot and rushed him out of the gym and in the direction of the boys' changing room. As they spilled through the door, Daisy wrinkled her nose in disgust.

'I think we've lost them,' she panted. 'Eww! What's that smell?'

'It's the boys,' Rose replied drily. 'Their changing room always smells like this.'

Rose immediately busied herself tapping more digits into her mobile.

'What are you doing?' asked Daisy. Couldn't Rose just talk to her seriously for once?

'Trying to communicate,' Rose said, oblivious to Daisy's increasingly agitated state. She handed the phone to the pint-sized alien.

'Well, try communicating with your own team first!' Daisy shouted, finally exploding. 'Do you know how much trouble we're in? We disobeyed orders!'

Lost for words, Rose stared at her co-agent. Daisy didn't look in the mood to hear her suspicions about Lenny!

Elsewhere in the building, the two Air One agents and their transponder unit finally arrived, followed closely by Carla and Lenny. But there was no sign of the M.I.9 agents in the gym. Instead, three flashing Pencil Communicators were abandoned on the floor.

Carla was apoplectic with rage. No pathetic kids

were going to interfere with her mission.

'So this is what you call thinking on your feet, is it?' she yelled at Lenny. 'Letting the fugitive escape?'

Lenny's face hardened. He'd taught Carla everything she knew. She had no right to talk to him like this.

'ASD3?' he spat back. 'So he's a *fugitive* now? We still haven't got all the facts.'

'The facts are that you knew how important it was that ASD3 was apprehended!' snapped Carla. She cursed under her breath. Events were spiralling out of her control and this had the potential to be a real disaster for her. With another quick glower at Lenny, Carla turned on her heels and stormed out of the gym. Her old mentor and the two Air One agents followed closely behind.

But despite finding evidence to the contrary, the Air One crew hadn't been alone in the gym. As they barrelled out of the room and back across the schoolyard, a face covered by dark floppy hair cautiously leaned out from his hiding place, high up on a window ledge.

It was Blane.

He'd heard the entire conversation and knew what they had to do.

Chapter 6

Back in the heart of St Hope's Park, Stewart and Colin had remained completely oblivious to the flurry of agent activity surrounding the crashed probe site. Stewart was leaping into a clearing, pointing excitedly. He'd just spied something *fantastic*.

'Look at that!' he cried, marvelling at the blackened patch of lawn that Daisy and Rose had discovered earlier. Colin hurried after him.

'Grass?' observed Colin.

'No!' Stewart replied, indicating the burnt area. 'Scorch marks. It means we're close. Which way through – left or right?'

'Ah, definitely right,' Colin decided. 'It's all about how objects ricochet on impact. I saw a documentary on the *Pseudo-Science Show*.'

Stewart was impressed. This Colin guy really knew his stuff. And together they made an *excellent* team. Stewart followed Colin willingly as they headed off in the exact opposite direction from where Rose and Daisy had found the spacecraft.

As he led his sidekick safely through an overgrown patch of blackberries, Colin decided he hadn't had so much fun since he'd last eaten a double bucket of popcorn at Cinema World.

'Whooohoo!' cheered Stewart, tugging excitedly at something he'd just spotted partially hidden under a bush. 'The UFO – we did it!'

Stewart triumphantly held up a football-sized metallic disc. A series of rivets were placed around its edges, and in its centre was a bronze dome. It was *clearly* alien technology.

'It's much smaller than I imagined,' murmured Colin, gazing at it with wonder. 'They must be shorter than us humans.'

'Let's get some photos,' said Stewart quickly, thrilled that he'd finally succeeded in snaring an extraterrestrial souvenir. 'We did it! We proved them all wrong!'

Colin pulled out his digital camera and was preparing to take a picture of the craft when he noticed something scratched into its surface.

'Hey, there's some writing,' he said, curiously rubbing some grime off the side. 'In English. "Hubble Roundabout Rides Ltd, Wakefield." Is it a code? What does it mean?'

Stewart looked at Colin in disappointment. *Not again!*

'It means we're idiots,' he said, shamefaced. 'That's what it means!'

Meanwhile, back in the changing rooms, the real secret agents were making a discovery of their own.

Blane had just burst in to tell the girls what he'd overheard – Carla and Lenny were searching for the alien and they'd given it a codename: ASD3.

Alarm bells went off in Rose's head. It was time to tell Daisy and Blane what she'd seen this morning.

'When I went back to get the last pod,' she recalled, 'Lenny was listening to a communiqué from Carla. It said how they were going to take ASD3 for examination – but I thought that meant part of the *probe*.'

But Daisy refused to believe Lenny wouldn't have their best interests at heart. 'Yeah, and what does *that* prove?' she asked.

'Lenny lied to us when he said the probe was unmanned,' Rose pointed out, her voice rising with concern. 'He *must* have known Air One were only interested in the pilot. And whatever they've got planned for him, I doubt it's a maths test!'

Blane agreed. Rose was right on this one.

But Daisy wasn't finished.

'Air One is a *government agency*,' she said, glaring at Rose. 'Two hours ago you were telling Stewart to *trust* the government! Now you're as big on conspiracy theories as he is!'

'GUYS!' Blane interjected, looking over their shoulders and watching in shock as something very strange started happening behind them. Following his gaze, the girls immediately stopped arguing and spun round.

The alien had been in the process of removing its helmet, just as Blane had shouted. And now here stood the last thing any of them had expected to see. A kid with dark straight hair and delicate features.

'It's a . . . boy!' Daisy gulped.

The pilot gave the three stunned agents a nervous smile.

'Greetings,' he said, speaking softly.

'He can talk like us!' gasped a stunned Daisy, still not quite believing he was human.

'I am Lu,' said the pilot in a foreign accent.

'Welcome, Lu,' said Rose, returning a friendly smile.

'I am test pilot,' Lu continued, concentrating hard. 'Er . . . chosen for mission because . . . because Lu expert in science. Er . . . Lu's mission peaceful. Only to see how craft fly.'

'But what about all that gunge?' asked Blane.

'Yeah,' added Daisy with an aggressive pout. There were still some things about Lu's story that bugged her. 'Humans leave *footprints*, not slime trails.'

'From fault,' replied Lu innocently. 'My ship crash because dimension stabilizer break.'

'That's my field!' beamed Rose. She was ignoring Daisy glowering at her. Rose sensed that she might have found a kindred spirit.

'You are scientist too?' asked the pilot with wonder.

Rose nodded her head in appreciation. At last – someone on the same wavelength!

But Daisy soon broke up their conversation. 'So, Lenny may have withheld some information. Big deal.'

'Face facts, Daisy,' said Rose curtly. 'He's *betrayed* us.'

'Is that all that loyalty means to you, Rose?' shouted Daisy, pushing aside Blane as he tried to calm her down. 'No wonder the only person who wants to talk to you is from another planet! We need Lenny's side of the story. Maybe they thought he was an alien too!'

Daisy turned stubbornly and headed for the door.

'You can't go,' shouted Blane, watching her retreating in dismay. 'In Air One's eyes, he's a fugitive . . . and so are you!'

Chapter 7

At the Air One base in the field behind the school, Carla and Lenny emerged from the blue van. Carla knew Lenny had always had a soft spot for her – and she was prepared to use that to her advantage.

'What your team don't know won't hurt them,' she insisted.

'I'm trusting you on this,' Lenny replied quietly. Carla's last sentence had sounded more like an order than a question. He was starting to think twice about this whole operation.

'I'd expect nothing less,' responded Carla coolly, before turning to a panel on the door of the van.

'Lock activation,' she said clearly. The locking system recognized her voice pattern and clicked shut.

Carla fixed her former boss with an icy stare. This was going to be harder than she thought.

* * *

As Lenny and Carla headed off into the distance, a head peered out from round the side of the trailer. It was a shocked Daisy, checking the coast was clear. She'd heard every word and suddenly felt dreadful for snapping at Rose all day – her fellow agent had been right after all. Lenny *was* keeping something from them! And now Daisy owed it to the rest of the team to uncover the truth.

She pulled out her MP3 player from her pocket. The moment Daisy had heard Carla pressuring Lenny, she'd hit the red 'record' button to replay the conversation to Blane and Rose later. And now it proved to be invaluable.

She held the device against the lock. Carla's voice sounded and the door clicked open.

Daisy hurried inside the trailer and pulled the door shut behind her. As her eyes adjusted to the eerie blue light, she couldn't help letting out a gasp. In the middle of the room was a medical table with two metallic wrist clamps on either side. Shining down on the bench was a bright spotlight, the kind that belonged in hospital operating theatres.

Beside the table was a unit set out with a row of sharp, gleaming surgical instruments.

Daisy felt her stomach turn. She'd obviously stumbled upon some macabre clinical experiment.

And then she spotted it. An opaque plastic wallet

containing some sort of document was on a side table by the bench. She snatched it and studied the writing on the front.

AIR ONE
SECRET DOCUMENT
HIGHLY CONFIDENTIAL
ASD/3 EUGENICS REPORT

Eugenics? Wasn't that genetic engineering? Daisy grimaced in shock. This was looking bad. *Really bad*.

But before she could read the rest of the document, footsteps sounded on the metal steps outside.

Daisy dived for cover behind a stretch of plastic sheeting hanging from the walls, her heart pounding.

A second later, Air One Agent 1 strode into the trailer. He stopped dead in his tracks. Something wasn't right – he could feel it.

Then he spotted the empty plastic wallet.

Emergency! In a flash, Agent 1 pressed a panel on the arm of his tight leather jacket. Hidden behind the sheeting, Daisy shuddered as an alarm shook the room.

'A blue room security breach!' Carla was shouting, a short distance away. 'I want a complete sweep of the area!'

From her hiding place, Daisy saw Agent 1 nod and immediately leave the room. She didn't know where he'd gone, but she had to get out of this horrible place right away.

She could hear Agent 1's voice coming from outside, relaying Carla's directions to his fellow Air One comrade.

Outside the trailer, the two agents were in full security mode. Agent 1 grabbed a pole and swivelled it in his hands in a slick kung-fu display.

Agent 2 smiled. He was relieved Carla had finally given them a trusted assignment and they could stay in the one spot. All this patrolling was causing him serious chafing.

As Agent 1 stopped his twirling, Agent 2 helpfully attached a brush to the end of the pole. Agent 1 nodded his thanks and set to work on the grass in front of the truck's metal steps.

Just as Carla had instructed – he was carrying out a 'sweep' of the area!

Over in the municipal park, Stewart was still smarting with disappointment at his non-find. How were they going to be famous UFO hunters when they couldn't even locate one that had crashed on their own doorstep?

'Look,' Colin said, interrupting Stewart's thoughts.

He was suddenly feeling very hungry. 'I've got this meal-for-one defrosting at home, but let's meet up tomorrow.'

'And resume the search?' said Stewart, perking up a little.

Colin nodded solemnly. Promising to ring Stewart in the morning, he walked back through the thicket. Despite their dud finds, Colin was satisfied with the day's events. With this Stewart kid on board, his uncle might even promote him to the top of that weird S.K.U.L. organization he was always going on about.

Having managed to sneak past the backs of the Air One agents as they concentrated on their cleaning, Daisy ran for the gym as fast as she could. Flying into the changing rooms, she revealed everything she had discovered to an incredulous Rose and Blane. Lenny was definitely onside with Carla Terrini and both had it in for Lu.

Blane was staring at the document Daisy had taken from the trailer.

'*Eugenics?*' he asked, raising a quizzical eyebrow.

'Genetic engineering to improve the human body,' Daisy explained with a rare spark of scientific knowledge. 'Lu is like the "new improved" version.'

'What?' shouted Rose. 'But he's just a kid, like us!'

'It's true,' Lu intercepted, dropping his shoulders in defeat. 'I was designed to be different . . . my cells . . . so my body can stand much G-force when craft fast.'

'Well, we're on your side now,' added Blane reassuringly.

'If we go against orders, it'll be the end of M.I. High,' said Rose sadly. They'd disobeyed instructions, destroyed hi-tech M.I.9 equipment and were now harbouring a fugitive. It didn't look good for any of them.

But seeing Lu's nervous face, they knew they just couldn't let Carla and her cronies take him to that trailer to be experimented on.

They were going to have to take on Carla Terrini together!

Chapter 8

Their new friend Lu needed a disguise. Something completely out of character so Air One would never find him . . .

After a quick rifle through the school lockers, Lu stood proudly in front of them in a maroon hoodie, a set of headphones and with a baseball cap pulled low over his face. His tiny frame was bent with the weight of the chunky, chavvy fake-gold chain hung round his neck.

They had raided the locker of St Hope's inept rapper, Fifty Pence.

Daisy eyed Lu's new outfit critically. She'd seen enough bad dress sense today, what with those Air One agents and their dreadful leather uniforms. And now *this*?

There was a commotion in the hallway and a clattering of footsteps. The agents glanced at each other. *Carla Terrini!*

'Seize them!' they heard Carla shout at her agents.

The fugitives pelted round a corner, but their escape plan was short-lived. The quartet crashed straight into a bizarrely outfitted Kenneth Flatley.

St Hope's eccentric Headmaster was wearing a straw hat with fake flowers on the top and a ribbon knotted neatly under his chin. He had abandoned his usual sensible brown suit for a colourful cardigan, with knee-length socks and shiny buckled shoes. He waved a pair of white handkerchiefs.

'Hello there,' Mr Flatley beamed, mistaking the shocked look on their faces for admiration. 'I expect you're all wondering why I'm dressed like this. Well, we've just finished the school morris-dancing class. Morris dancing is becoming very popular again, you know.'

His interlude ground to a halt as Carla and her agents came speeding round the corner.

'Oh, hello!' chirped Mr Flatley. 'More new faces! I'm afraid you're too late for this afternoon's class.'

Carla's top lip quivered in contempt. *Who was this idiot?* Carla collared Lu and pulled him towards her.

But Daisy wasn't about to let Lu be taken back to that horrible room. She grabbed the handkerchiefs from Mr Flatley and began to sing, performing a strange hopping dance: *'Wave your hankies left and right. Wear those leggings really tight!'*

Skipping over to Carla, Daisy snatched Lu from

her grasp and ushered him towards her *own* fellow agents.

Carla glowered at her. *What a pitiful attempt.* In five years of the Young Spy Awards she'd *never* had to resort to morris dancing.

'Never mind about that!' Carla shouted, taking on the fake persona of Lu's cockney mum with a less than convincing accent. 'What's my boy doing out 'ere so late?' She leaned over and pulled at Lu.

'He's here for morris-dancing classes!' trilled Daisy through gritted teeth, grabbing Lu back.

'Not with 'is bad knee, he 'ain't!' Carla yelled, still pretending to be Lu's mum and dragging him towards her.

'Well, he can still wave his *arms*!' shouted Daisy firmly, moving over and flapping Lu's arms in the air to demonstrate.

Mr Flatley frowned. If this boy really was physically incapacitated, then it was his duty as Headmaster to implement St Hope's health and safety policy.

'There's no way that poor boy can perform with an injury,' he declared vigilantly. 'Our routines are very vigorous!'

The Headmaster took Lu tightly by the arm and passed him back to Carla, who flashed the three teen spies a smirk of satisfaction. Daisy shivered. She'd never seen such a beautiful woman look so evil.

Mr Flatley watched oblivious as Carla and her two agents hurried off, dragging a petrified Lu with them.

'How marvellous to see parents taking an interest too, eh?' he observed, sighing with contentment.

As he pranced off down the corridor, belting out a rousing chorus of 'Hey Nonny, Hey Nonny, Hey No', the M.I. High agents looked at each other in utter disbelief.

How on *earth* were they going to save Lu now?

Chapter 9

A terrified Lu was laid out on the operating table in the Air One trailer. The tiny pilot craned his neck to look down at the metallic wrist clamps. Lu tried to struggle but his arms wouldn't move. It was hopeless.

'Lu's mission peaceful,' he insisted, his eyes looking widely at the agents surrounding him.

'Be quiet!' snapped Carla aggressively.

Lenny and Carla stood on opposite sides of the table. Lenny's face was twisted in fury.

'You never told me you were dealing with a *child*,' he snapped angrily.

'He's the product of a foreign power's eugenics programme,' Carla replied dismissively. 'Age is irrelevant. It's our duty to investigate.'

'You call this an investigation?' Lenny yelled in dismay. 'The Carla I knew would never have allowed it.'

Lu moaned on the table. Carla watched him coldly, choosing to ignore his obvious distress.

'I have my orders,' she said, looking back at Lenny with an icy stare.

'And I have my conscience,' Lenny replied, looking at her curiously. Was she challenging him? 'The boy has no place here.'

'The world has changed, Lenny,' Carla said with condescending menace. 'You are with us on this one, aren't you?'

'I know where my duty lies, yes,' Lenny replied, inhaling deeply. He hoped he sounded more convinced than he felt.

'Good!' snapped Carla, relieved to have her old mentor back on board. 'The interrogation begins in ten minutes. I want you there.'

Outside, Daisy was again cautiously approaching the Air One van, this time backed up by Blane. Agent 1 was standing near the van's open door, guarding the vehicle.

Daisy pulled out her MP3 player and tossed it towards the grass, several metres from Agent 1's position. Landing with a soft thud, the 'play' button triggered automatically.

Agent 1 looked around in puzzlement as the sound of Carla's voice echoed from somewhere near the side of the van.

'*Lock activation*,' it said.

Agent 1 scratched his head. He couldn't *see* his boss anywhere, but he could certainly hear her. The agent wandered off to investigate.

With the van unguarded, Daisy and Blane quickly crept inside. Daisy gasped at the pitiful sight of Lu on the table. They rushed over, attempting to pull the pilot's arms free, but the wrist clamps wouldn't budge.

As the martial arts expert of the M.I. High team, Blane took charge. He smashed through the first and then the second clamp. Both sprang open immediately.

Blane and Daisy helped the dazed Lu off the table. They had to get out of there as soon as possible. But as they reached the exit, three tall figures appeared.

'Well, what do we have here?' spat Carla venomously. 'Lenny's tiny-tot spies?'

As Daisy, Blane and Lu backed nervously into the trailer, Carla hurled herself towards the door. But as she reached the steps, the van's engine suddenly revved into life and the whole vehicle pulled away at high speed. Unable to successfully pull herself into the trailer, Carla soared through the air and hit the field with a *THUMP*, as the two teen agents and pilot were thrown to the floor inside.

'M.I.9 are now expendable!' Carla screeched at

her Air One agents, barking orders as she lay on the ground. 'Follow them!'

As the van careered across the field, Blane and Daisy rushed to the front to investigate. They pushed open the small door dividing the main room from the driver's cab and saw an unexpected but familiar face . . .

'Lenny?' gasped Blane with amazement.

'Don't worry, I'm on your side!' Lenny shouted, driving like a madman. 'I just had to keep Carla on board until I knew her plans!'

Daisy pulled a grin of relief. Of course Lenny wouldn't let them down!

Lenny yanked down on the steering wheel and the trailer screeched out of the school's side driveway. They were heading in the direction of St Hope's Park.

Chapter 10

Rose had sprinted all the way to the crashed aircraft site. She needed to fix the space probe for Lu.

She found it, just as they'd left it. Rose lifted the domed lid and gingerly climbed into the pilot's seat. In her hands, she held the dimensional stabilizer she'd built for her science project. Inserting her invention into a gap in the panel, Rose sighed with relief as it slotted in perfectly.

Now it just had to actually work. Holding her breath, Rose connected two of her stabilizer's wires together.

'*Come on, come on!*' she urged, looking down frantically as lights and buttons flickered on the flight panel.

'The stabilizer . . .' a voice said suddenly. 'You repair?'

Rose looked up to find Lu crouching down beside the craft, holding his helmet under his arm. The two friends greeted each other with huge grins, as Blane,

Daisy and Lenny looked on. Rose could see that M.I. High were a team again.

'Not quite,' Rose said hesitantly. 'I had to use my own instead. It's only a prototype, though. I'm worried it might not work.'

'You give me your project?' Lu whispered in hushed gratitude. 'With this, you could be famous!'

'Science is about more than reputations,' Rose replied stoically, climbing out of the craft. 'Now hurry!'

Just metres away, the M.I.9 crew watched in amusement as Carla and her cronies reached the first orange pod. Agents 1 and 2 dashed forward, smacking straight into the force field and flying backwards.

'Headbangers!' grinned Blane, chuckling.

Lu hurried into the pilot seat as Rose knelt down beside the cockpit. She could feel a lump rising in her throat.

'Good luck, Lu,' she smiled. 'I'm sorry I didn't get to know you better.'

'Maybe one day we meet at science conference?' Lu asked eagerly.

'I hope so,' agreed Rose, as they touched hands.

Inside, Lu flicked a button on the flight panel and slipped on his helmet. The domed lid of the craft flipped smoothly shut as the engine roared to life.

'I hope he makes it,' said Daisy, waving as the small craft rose towards the sky.

Elsewhere in the park, Stewart was walking home, a glum expression on his face. He'd stayed on after Colin left, but he was no closer to finding any extraterrestrials.

Suddenly, a round metallic disc rose into the air in front of him. It was exactly like one he'd seen that morning. The UFO was back! Not taking his eyes off the craft, a trembling Stewart quickly pulled out his mobile phone.

But before he could click the button to take a photo, the ship changed direction and suddenly zigzagged towards him. He had to dive out of the way to avoid being hit by the speeding craft.

By the time a shaken Stewart clambered to his feet, it had gone.

Chapter 11

At the crash site, Blane, Daisy, Rose and Lenny continued to watch with interest as the two hapless Air One agents tried to dismantle the force field. After several minutes of rummaging through a bag of assorted wires, Agents 1 and 2 finally managed to disable a small section of the invisible shield.

'Arrest them!' Carla demanded the instant they broke through, pointing an accusatory finger at Lenny and his team.

'That wouldn't be wise,' Lenny tutted, scolding her like a young child. 'The probe is leaving our airspace approximately . . .'

He glanced down at his watch.

'. . . now. And according to M.I.9 rules on agency procedure – clause eight, sub-section nine – Air One no longer has jurisdiction over me *or* my team.'

'So clear off!' added Daisy from behind the safety of Lenny's shoulder.

Carla snorted with a mix of frustration and rage.

There was nothing more she could do. Except thump her two useless Air One agents as she stormed from the park.

Colin was chattering animatedly on his mobile, eating a choc-chip cookie.

'Chill out, Unc!' he said brightly. 'We might have lost the probe thingy, but at least I got to meet Agent Stewart!'

'Who?' demanded the Grand Master. 'I don't remember any Stewart on the files.'

'Who?' Colin repeated, incensed. 'What do you mean *who*? He's only the best agent S.K.U.L. ever had.'

'I can't take any more of this!' groaned the Grand Master, despairing at his nephew's stupidity. 'I'm going to spend a week in my holiday bunker under the Indian Ocean.'

'Er – could I be in charge until you get back?' asked Colin hopefully, sensing a career opportunity.

'Certainly not!' snapped the Grand Master, gazing down at the giant white rabbit sitting in his lap. 'General Flopsy will cover. I need someone with a *brain*.'

Lenny was thrilled with his team's performance. Unlike Carla Terrini, his young agents had proved they knew right from wrong.

'No more secrets between us, eh?' smiled Lenny, watching the sunlit horizon as Lu's craft finally disappeared from view.

'But we're spies,' pointed out Blane, grinning at his mentor. 'Isn't keeping secrets what we do?'

'Not from each other,' cut in Rose, offering her fellow agent an apologetic shrug. 'Daisy was right – for once.'

'Well,' Daisy teased, in Rose's defence, 'I shouldn't have been mean about your boyfriend.'

'He's *not* my–' Rose stopped in mid-sentence as she noticed Daisy trying to stifle a snigger. What was the point?

'Come on,' said Lenny, once again the authority figure of M.I. High. 'Let's get these pods shifted before some poor dog gets five thousand volts up his choke chain!'

Blane began to laugh, but the sight of a figure frozen in its tracks only a few metres away made him gulp audibly.

At the entrance to the clearing, Stewart's eyes were out on stalks. Not only had a UFO just very nearly flattened him, but there – right in front of him – was his best friend Blane, dressed in a sleek black uniform. And there were Daisy Millar and Rose Gupta too, kitted out in the same gear. And what on *earth* was Lenny the school caretaker doing with them, wearing a crisp immaculate dinner suit?

Stewart rubbed his eyes. They all looked like secret agents!

'Blane?' he called out.

Sprinting forward, Stewart ran full pelt into the force field. Like the Air One agents before him, he fell, stunned, to the ground.

When Stewart came to, he found Blane, Daisy and Rose looking anxiously down at him. Stewart frowned. They were all dressed in their school uniforms and Lenny was nowhere to be seen.

'It's OK, you've just had a bit of a shock,' explained Blane, helping him up.

'Yeah, it was so weird,' Stewart muttered, rubbing his head and blinking wildly. 'I thought I saw a UFO and then you dressed as . . . like . . . *spies*.'

'Spies!' laughed Rose, a little too hysterically.

'Us?' added Daisy, fixing Stewart with a look that left no doubt as to how much of a weirdo she thought he was. 'As if!'

Having said their goodbyes, Stewart smiled as the four friends walked out of St Hope's Park and headed for home. He'd decided not to tell Blane about his meeting with Colin. He didn't want him to get jealous.

Besides, he didn't think Blane would ever believe him when he told him secret agents really did exist!

Puffin by Post

M.I. High: Secrets and Spies

If you have enjoyed this book and want to read more,
then check out these other great Puffin titles.
You can order any of the following books direct with Puffin by Post:

M.I. High: A New Generation • 9780141323619	£4.99
Join Daisy, Blane and Rose in two amazing action-packed episodes from the BBC series.	
The Official M.I. High Spy Survival Handbook • 9780141323633	£3.99
Enter the world of M.I.9 with character profiles, exciting gadgets and mission briefs.	
SilverFin • Charlie Higson • 978014131859	£6.99
'Good, gritty and funny . . . Very clever, Bond, very clever indeed' – *Daily Mail*	
Hurricane Gold • Charlie Higson • 9780141383910	£12.99
'Double-oh so good' – *Sunday Times*	
The Devil's Breath • David Gilman • 9780141323022	£6.99
'Heart-pounding action' – *The Times*	

Just contact:

Puffin Books, C/o Bookpost, PO Box 29,
Douglas, Isle of Man, IM99 1BQ
Credit cards accepted. For further details:
Telephone: 01624 677237
Fax: 01624 670923

You can email your orders to: bookshop@enterprise.net
Or order online at: www.bookpost.co.uk

Free delivery in the UK.
Overseas customers must add £2 per book.

Prices and availability are subject to change.

Visit puffin.co.uk to find out about the latest titles, read extracts and
exclusive author interviews, and enter exciting competitions.
You can also browse thousands of Puffin books online.